Death Rides Alone

When Bronco Travis rides into the mining town of Silverton in Colorado Territory, his only thought is to avenge the death of his father. Nobody recognizes the young son of the part-time marshal who had been brutally murdered eight years before by Jack Bowdrie and his gang. It appeared straightforward enough: just slip into town and get the job done.

But Bowdrie has taken over the town and has no intention of being ousted from his profitable roost. So when the bodies begin to pile up, the gang boss takes swift action that almost ends in Bronco's own demise.

He will need all his wits and a lethal gun-hand if his deadly nemesis is to be defeated.

Death Rides Alone

Dale Graham

A Black Horse Western

ROBERT HALE · LONDON

© Dale Graham 2005
First published in Great Britain 2005

ISBN 0 7090 7854 4

Robert Hale Limited
Clerkenwell House
Clerkenwell Green
London EC1R 0HT

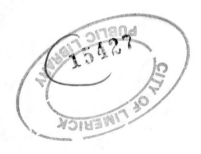
Typeset by
Derek Doyle & Associates, Shaw Heath.
Printed and bound in Great Britain by
Antony Rowe Limited, Wiltshire.

ONE

RETURN TO SILVERTON

Cresting a low rise, the solitary rider drew his chestnut mount to a halt. Like a prowling cougar, he surveyed the once-familiar terrain. All around, jutting peaks vied for attention, their naked bones still mailed in ice, even in July. Nudging the horse forward he paused a second time, just inside the lonely Hillside Cemetery that overlooked the town of Baker's Park in central Colorado.

The broken gate hung askew on a single rusty hinge. Untended, the graves lay sad and forlorn, abandoned to the elements. A bleak look riveted on to a lichen-coated marker bearing the epitaph:

Henry Coward:
Shot dead on Blair Street
for doing his duty
15 May 1869.
Rest in Peace

Dark-grey eyes, brittle and ice-cold lay deep in shadow, hidden beneath the wide brim of a battered Plainsman. The man stepped down, removed the hat and held it tightly with both hands in front of his gunbelt. The bone handle of a Colt Frontier poked out from a cross-draw holster. Head bowed, the tight lips moved ever so slightly, offering a silent prayer to the deceased.

Eight years had passed since he had stood in this very same spot, desperately clutching his mother's trembling hand.

A single teardrop etched a pained furrow down the tanned visage, a face that appeared young yet exuded more heartache than anyone that young could be expected to bear.

Silence, grim and austere, broken only by the gentle sough of a low breeze, permeated the small graveyard. But only for a moment before a sinister echo bounced off the decaying tombstones. It was a discordant sound, out of place in this peaceful locale – the deadly click-click of a rotating cylinder as the stranger checked the loading of his well-oiled six-shooter.

Flicking the tear from his eye, as if guilty at showing such emotion, the young stranger brushed a stray lock of dark hair from his forehead, re-set his hat and mounted up. Only then did he fasten a stoical gaze on to the town below.

His demeanour hardened, once again resuming the tough exterior of a man inured to the demanding ways of the frontier. Baker's Park had altered immeasurably since his departure a little over eight years past following the untimely demise of his father.

The single main street was now twice its original length. A host of side roads branched off giving it the appearance of a giant chess-board. And clustered around the edges, a chaotic array of white canvas tents littered the valley floor. Gamely they struggled for acceptance in the buzzing metropolis.

A throbbing hum reached the young man's ears.

'Seems like things have changed some around here, Blaze,' he muttered to his horse. The animal flicked its ears in agreement, emitting a compressed snort. 'OK, I know,' responded the rider, patting the side of its head, 'You ain't the only one in need of solid meal and a bed for the night.'

The sun beat down with unrestrained fury. Only a few stray wisps of cloud offered any resistance to the torrid heat. The man untied his necker and carefully wiped a sweat-stained brow. He uncorked a water bottle, sprinkled the necker with the precious fluid and dabbed the horse's nose before tipping the remaining contents down his own parched gullet.

A myth often assumed by lowlanders was that the high valleys were a lot colder than the plains. Certainly in winter the snows could find Old Nick shivering his socks off. But at this time of year, there was little wind to disperse the heat from the sheltered valleys.

He nudged the chestnut gently with his knees, guiding her out of the cemetery and down the winding trail towards the huddle of buildings below. As they neared the eastern limit of settlement, piles of abandoned debris, the residue of high-profile mining activity, loomed head high on either side of the narrow rutted highway. And in this heat, to describe the smell as ripe was a distinct understatement. The stranger gave a barking cough as the stench bit deep.

Bearded miners hammered at the rough earth with picks while their partners avidly shovelled heaps of loose gravel into the long toms. Feverish looks of expectation that a major strike was theirs for the taking suffused the weary faces. Few bothered to note the arrival of a new face. Just one more prospector hoping to strike it rich.

The rider hauled rein and casually addressed the nearest miner. An old jasper busily sifting the tailings at the riffled end of the long-tom sluice paused.

'Hit pay-dirt yet?' asked the newcomer.

A suspicious look creased the rumpled visage.

'Maybe,' came back the reserved comment. 'Then again, maybe not.' It didn't do for a man to advertise any success he might have had. Too many others had been found down a back alley with a shiv stuck in their gut after announcing a rich strike to the world.

'Just that there's a heap of work goin' on around this berg, is all,' offered the newcomer, sensing the other's reticence.

'That's 'cos there's bin a new strike of silver at this end of the valley, if you hadn't noticed,' responded the miner with a bite of sarcasm. Nevada Jones took the meeting as a welcome opportunity to rest from his labours. 'New prospectors bin arrivin' every day,' The old-timer grunted disdainfully. 'But all the best claims have been staked if it's easy pickings you're after. Try Ouray over Red Mountain Pass.' He casually flipped a thumb towards the north end of the valley. 'Rumour has it there's bin a fresh strike over there. We'll be headin' that way ourselves if these diggin's run dry.'

It was clear that the miner didn't welcome anybody muscling in on his claim.

'I ain't no prospector, that's fer dang sure,' reacted the young man tersely. 'It's a mug's game if'n you ask me.'

'Nobody did, mister.'

Other miners on neighbouring claims had stopped to listen to the exchange. Bent backs straightened, tense with expectation.

The kid peered around, a cautious glint in his eye. He had no wish to have his visit terminated before he'd even arrived. Nor did he welcome the attention his caustic remark was attracting. Silently he cursed his quick temper. On too many occasions in the past it had bubbled over, leading to unwelcome complications.

He pulled his hat low over the darkly stubbled face, realizing he had to tread carefully.

'No offence, feller.' He apologized with a strained attempt at mollification. 'Just passin' through.' Then he quickly aimed a conciliatory question at the man. 'Now where can a thirsty traveller wash the trail dust from his gizzard?' An edgy laugh issued from compressed lips.

Their eyes locked. Age versus youth. A casual smile split the miner's weather-beaten contours. Uneven teeth yellowed by constant baccy-chewing were revealed. Nevada Jones visibly relaxed.

'Try the Bent Elbow,' he offered. 'Just follow your nose down the middle of Blair Street. You can't miss it.' The old guy aimed a finger down into the main huddle of clapboard shacks before asking: 'What they call you then, kid?'

'The name's Bronco Travis,' replied the newcomer, nudging his horse forward. 'I've been bustin' wild horses up around the Wind River in Wyoming for the last six months. Much obliged to you.'

In fact, Bronco had earned his nickname through being the youngest rider to break ten horses a day on a consistent basis. But that wasn't the end of the job. It then took a further five days to train the string to the high standard demanded by the cavalry selection committee. That was something even the regular busters struggled to achieve.

By his third week with the outfit, Vince Cole, the top wrangler, had figured him as a natural. So George Travis was christened 'Bronco'. It had been one of the proudest moments of his young life. But after six gruelling months of rising at the grey light of dawn and not finishing until after sunset, Bronco was feeling the strain. No job could have been tougher.

And it was more due to luck than good judgement that he had escaped serious injury. As the saying went. *There ain't no horse that can't be rode, and there ain't no man that can't be throwed.* It was a true enough adage.

But a poignant remark uttered by one of the hands eventually made up his mind to quit while he was still on top, so to speak.

'Take my advice Bronco,' advised his friend, 'Few bronc riders ever pass thirty. More'n likely they end up getting kicked into a funeral procession.'

Having drawn his pay, the kid had lit out the next day.

'Yep!' he reiterated casting a critical eye over the untidy settlement, 'Baker's Park sure has changed.'

Before Bronco had time to gig his mount forward the old miner spoke again.

'How long you bin away?' he asked. Not waiting for a reply, the old guy continued: ' 'Cos things have changed more'n you figure.' Nevada Jones paused with a smirk breaking across his weathered features. The comment was backed up by a chorus of ribald guffawing from his cronies.

Bronco eased back the reins. a puzzled look on his face.

'What you warblin' about, old man?' A touch of impatience had once again crept into the kid's reaction.

'Either you're in the wrong place. Or you bin away above a coon's age. And seeing as you ain't more'n a kid—'

'Just spit it out, will yuh?' interrupted Bronco curtly, squaring his shoulders.

'This here's Silverton! Silverton, y'hear?' crowed Jones

slapping his thigh, 'Leastways it's bin that way ever since I packed in a year ago.' He turned to his partner for confirmation. 'Ain't that the goldarned truth, Jim?'

Another grizzled veteran shovelling gravel at the top end of the sluice grunted without pausing in his labours. The chance of striking that elusive bonanza always assumed precedence over everything.

Bronco took that as an affirmative.

'Don't mind Old Virginity,' chortled Jones, eyeing his partner askance. 'He's just a tetchy old sourpuss.' He pointed a finger to his head, rolling his eyes. The meaning was obvious. The oldster gave a rabid cackle.

'Old Virginny's a sourpuss! Old Virginny's a sourpuss!' he sang out.

Veteran of mining-camps too numerous to mention, Jim Finney (known throughout the Rockies as 'Old Virginny') scowled at the newcomer. Ever since he'd been cheated out of a rightful share in the now famous Comstock Lode by Henry Comstock himself back in 1860, Jim had placed his trust in nobody. Excepting 'Old Betsy' that is, a Hawken long rifle that never left his side.

When others enquired after his success or otherwise, Jim Finney always took the opportunity to disparage his ex-partner's chicanery, the assertion being that his share of the fortune had been tricked out of him after a heavy bout of drinking.

'Took me for a sucker, did Comstock,' was the invariable waspish comment. 'He had a tongue as silvery as the diggings. Bought my share for naught but a bottle of cheap booze and a blind horse.' The ribald cackling that inevitably followed this tale did nothing to assuage Finney's bitterness.

Nevada Jones clucked, then added: 'Old Man Baker died

in the cholera outbreak of '75. That's when the latest ore strike was made and the camp became known as Silverton.'

'Silverton or Baker's Park. Makes no difference to me. This is the right place, sure enough,' crackled Bronco.

'What's your business in Silverton then, Travis?'

Bronco laid his gaze on his rapt audience. Scanning the assemblage, he mumbled almost incoherently:

'Just some unfinished business that needs tying up.'

Then he spurred the chestnut away from the babble of comment at his back.

Care and patience were needed to pick his way along the rutted trail leading into the broad thoroughfare of the town. Stunned by the cacophony of sound that assailed his ears, Bronco hunched down into his light buckskin jacket, slowing the feisty Blaze to a steady walk.

The street was heaving.

Freight hauliers, their wagons piled high with pit-props and sawn timber held the centre, while horse-riders took the edge, carelessly pushing aside anybody foolish enough to get in their way. Cattle heading for the slaughterhouse at the far end of town heedlessly bludgeoned everybody in their path. And pedestrians stepping off the wooden boardwalks to cross the busy concourse took their lives in their hands.

This was Silverton – 1877. And definitely no Baker's Park.

Before he had left with his mother, eight years back, the town had been a quiet, sleepy, some might even say dull settlement. Nothing ever happened to break the gentle pace of life. The town did not even have its own law officer. That was until his father was persuaded against his better judgement to take on the job.

The reason for his presence in Silverton suddenly hit the young stranger like a slap in the face. His expression took on the umbered hue of an approaching thunder-storm. Frown lines creased his brow. Deep-set grey eyes, dark and brooding, recalled the dire sequence of events that had changed his life for ever that May afternoon back in 1869. On that fateful day, Bronco Travis had lost for ever his youthful innocence, his unbridled zest for life.

Horror-stricken at the abrupt confrontation that had violently terminated his father's life, the initial pain and shock had festered over the coming years to be replaced by a burning thirst for vengeance against the perpetrators.

'Them murderin' sons-of-bitches are gonna pay dear for what they done to me and mine,' he heard himself muttering into the ears of the chestnut. 'You pay heed to what I'm sayin', Blaze. This town will rue the day that Bronco Travis came a-callin'.' The horse trembled invol-untarily, sensing the fierce tension squeezing at the innards of her young master.

A lone buzzard flew past cawing and flapping its large black wings before settling on the roof of one of numer-ous false-fronted establishments lining the busy street. Bronco eyed the flyer, a macabre omen of things to come. A couple more soon joined their comrade, bloodthirsty predators watching the newcomer and perhaps sensing a hint of gladiatorial sport in the air. Bronco chewed on his lower lip, a sneer of disdain effectively removing any hint of youthful virtue that might have lingered.

Lowering his gaze, the kid noted that the building opposite was a livery stable. The legend *Ben Murphy – horse trader to the discerning rider* was emblazoned in green letter-ing across the front. Bronco badly needed sustenance, but the chestnut was more important. She always took first place in the queue.

He stepped down and led the sweating animal into the

cool interior of the barn, noting the tidy arrangement of the stalls and equipment. A place for everything, and everything in its place. Ben Murphy was obviously a man who cared about his work. Blaze would be well looked after here.

'Hello!' The call echoed round the plank walls. 'Anybody home.'

No reply was forthcoming.

The kid removed the heavy saddle and tied the lead rein to a post. Then he went in search of the elusive owner. The office at the rear was open but empty. Bronco shrugged. He would help himself to oats for his horse and fix the chestnut up with a stall. He could settle the bill later, after he'd seen to his own needs at the Bent Elbow.

After reassuring the horse, Bronco was about to head off down to the saloon.

An alien sound to his rear caused the kid to whirl on his heel. In a blur of speed that took less than a blink of the eye, the Frontier Colt leapt into his right hand. The ugly snout poked with menacing intent at the midriff of a tall, grey-haired man clutching a twin-pronged hay-fork.

'A man shouldn't oughta creep up on another like that, mister,' said Bronco coolly, his thumb curled around the cocked hammer of the deadly pistol. 'Feller could get hisself shot full of holes.'

In his mid-forties, the man was lean and clean-shaven with leather suspenders holding up a pair of brown whipcord pants. The open shirt revealed a well-muscled torso. He was sweating hard – and not from any perceived danger. This guy was no stranger to hard graft.

He held his ground, not in the slightest unnerved by the kid's threatening stance. A piercing gaze met the younger man's stare evenly. That was when Bronco noticed the three-inch scar down the left side of the ostler's tanned face. An insipid yellow, it gave the man a permanent scowl. A once-handsome face ruined.

'This is my establishment,' replied the ostler steadily. 'The name's Ben Murphy. And folks usually ask before taking it upon themselves to use my facilities.'

Bronco slowly and purposefully eased down the hammer, stepped back and slid the weapon back into its holster.

'Sorry about that, Mr Murphy,' he sighed. 'Couldn't find nobody to ask.'

Murphy relaxed, placing the fork aside. 'I was out back unloading some fresh hay for the bedding.'

'Sure appears like a well-run livery.'

'That's very kind of you, sir.'

This response to Bronco's compliment came from an unexpected source to his left. A flaxen-haired girl clad in check shirt and a split leather riding-skirt stood framed in the open doorway. A broad-brimmed Stetson was pushed to the back of her head. With an easy grace she led a black stallion into the stable.

Bronco couldn't help noticing the trim narrow waist, the hips swaying like a mesmerized cobra. Wavy hair like a ripening cornfield flowed down her back. She was indeed a sight for the proverbial sore eyes, and the first young female he had encountered for over half a year.

His lower jaw dragged on the dusty floor.

The girl tethered her mount and peered at the young man through deep emerald-green eyes.

'Cat gotten your tongue then?' she queried, a wry smile lighting up the alabaster complexion.

To save the boy from embarrassment, Ben Murphy made the introductions.

'This is my daughter, Ellen. She's been visiting a friend over in Eureka, a small town up the valley.'

'Pleased to meet you Mr. . . ?'

'Well . . . erm . . .'

'Forgotten your name then?' The girl's hypnotic eyes were playing a dangerous game with Bronco's rampant emotions.

'Name's . . . er . . . Bronco, Bronco Travis, ma'am,' he stammered grabbing his hat from atop the unruly thatch of black hair. 'Just arrived in town and I need a good stable for Blaze.' Ellen Murphy's eyes lifted questioningly. He pointed absently over to the middle stall where the horse was nuzzling contentedly on the bag of oats.

Father and daughter glanced over. Instantly, their backs stiffened. Ellen emitted a startled gasp.

'You can't leave it there.' The girl's sharp reaction was laced with fear.

Bronco gave her a quizzical frown. Ben Murphy cleared his throat before answering. 'That there stall is reserved,' he muttered, shuffling his feet uneasily.

Bronco peered from one to the other. Both were jumpy and anxious.

'Why can't this joker take the one next to it?' retorted Bronco, shaking his head. 'My cayuse is all settled now.'

'Mr Bowdrie wouldn't take kindly to that.'

Bronco staggered back a pace. He looked as if he'd been struck in the face. His jaw tightened. A cold glint regarded the ostler.

'That wouldn't be Jack Bowdrie, would it?' prodded the young man, 'Known as Flat Nose by friend and foe alike?'

'The very same!' exclaimed a surprised Ben Murphy. 'You and him acquainted?'

Bronco ignored the question.

'So Bowdrie is still here,' he murmured to himself before addressing the livery man again. 'How long you been in Silverton, Mr Murphy?'

'We arrived here back in the spring of '70.'

Bronco nodded. One year after he and his mother had left. Forced out by Bowdrie and his gang of toughs.

'Well you inform *Mister* Bowdrie when he calls by that I'm commandeering that stall,' growled Bronco, drawing himself up, fists clenched tightly. 'And he can go jump at the moon.' He flipped a double-eagle to the ostler. 'Be stayin' a week at least. If the charge is any more let me know.'

'You have some kind of quarrel with Bowdrie, Mr Travis?' enquired an anxious Ellen Murphy.

'You could say that we don't quite see eye to eye, ma'am.'

The flushed hint of anger spreading across the bronc-buster's countenance told a different tale.

'Jack Bowdrie is a dangerous man to tangle with,' interjected Murphy bitterly. 'And I should know.'

Ellen gripped her father's arm. The older man paused in his flow, voice subdued, the inflection wavering. He grasped his daughter's hand.

'Go on, Mr Murphy,' said Bronco quietly. 'I'm all ears.'

'Well,' he began. 'Everything was OK for the first six months. Business was picking up nicely. Then one morning, Bowdrie stopped by. Suggested that I needed insurance against what he called – unexpected outcomes. And if I didn't agree to his terms, he hinted that accidents might start to happen.' Murphy rubbed his hands together and gave a deep sigh. He was clearly on edge. 'I laughed in his face. Told him I'd decide when and if I needed help.'

He paused wiping the beads of perspiration from his brow. 'It was two days later that it happened.'

'It's all right, dad,' whispered Ellen Murphy, patting her father's hand. 'You don't have to do this.'

Murphy shrugged her off, his eyes blank and staring.

'Three of my horses had their throats cut. When I protested to Bowdrie, he pistol-whipped me in the middle of Blair Street. In front of the whole town. Just to show everybody who was running things.' His hand strayed to the long pale furrow down his left cheek. Then he sat down on a barrel, shaking his head.

Tears laced Ellen Murphy's face as she tried to console her distraught father. Then she turned to the cause of all this grief.

'Why can't you just take another stall and save us all a heap of trouble,' she cried. 'Just leave us alone.'

Bronco could feel her pain. He knew only too well the hurt that Flat Nose Jack Bowdrie was capable of inflicting, just for the hell of it. But he had no intention of backing down to that dog's-breath.

No way!

'Tell that low-down sneaking coyote that Bronco Travis is in town, and waiting on his pleasure at the Bent Elbow. That oughta get him out of your hair in double-quick time. I ain't here to cause you folks any trouble. It's with Bowdrie that I have scores to settle.'

Then he hitched up his gunbelt and strode resolutely out into the late-afternoon sun. Ellen Murphy followed him to the door.

'Watch your back, Mr Travis,' she called with feeling. 'That turkey is as slippery as a wet fish.'

The young man raised a hand in acknowledgement but didn't look back.

TWO

STIRRING THE POT

It was easy to find the Bent Elbow. The problem was reaching it from the opposite side of the street. If it wasn't the never-ending stream of traffic, then the deep water-filled ruts offered their own unique brand of bedevilment.

Eventually he made it. The thought passed through his mind that perhaps this town would benefit from the new stop-go lighting system he'd read about which was now operating in Chicago.

But first a long cool drink. His throat felt like the inside of a wagon driver's glove.

Shouldering through the batwing doors, Bronco stepped into the twilight world of the Bent Elbow. He purposefully filtered into the shadows, surveying the various occupants of the long, narrow room. At this early hour, there was only a handful of drinkers. Two cowhands stood at the bar, their leather chaps clearly announcing their occupation. A piano-player in the corner desperately attempted to coax a tune from his battered instrument. And over on the right, a couple of games were in progress.

The garish red-silk vest sported by one named him as the house gambler.

But it was the three well-dressed gents in the end alcove who attracted Bronco's attention. He squinted through the dim light cast by a coal-oil lamp, giving them a second eyeful. Just to make sure.

Dan Tanner! He didn't cotton to the other two. He nodded in an expressive manner. Greyer with sagging jowls, they proudly wore the padded bellies typical of the successful businessmen they clearly had become. Yes, indeed. This supercilious buzzard had come up in the world. It was Tanner who had been leader of the town council when his father was killed.

And it was Tanner who had failed miserably in his civic duty of care.

Bronco scowled, his mouth an ugly slash as the lurid memories flooded back.

And neither you, nor the rest of the good citizens of Baker's Park, had lifted a finger to help, he mused. The notion to confront this vile object of his revulsion here and now was overwhelming. He made to approach, gun-hand flexing.

Just in time, he held back.

Not yet awhile. His time would come.

Thankfully nobody took any notice of the newcomer. It was eight years since, and he had changed radically during the interim. From a gawky sprout of fourteen, he had matured into a hard-bitten missionary of vengeance. The men had glanced across and immediately labelled him as a no-account drifter. That was how he wanted it.

Shambling up to the bar, he was immediately approached by a thin weasel boasting a spindly moustache. Thinning black hair was plastered to his skull and parted dead centre. A false smile appeared on the barkeep's oily features.

'What'll it be, mister?'

'Beer,' grunted Bronco, 'and make it ice-cold. None of that tepid muck you foist on to the miners.'

The barkeep's smile disappeared. A scowl replaced it. More like your normal demeanour, thought Bronco. He knew bartenders – and their slimy ways.

'We only serve the finest brews in this establishment,' sniffed the weasel, known universally by the appellation of King Arthur – a reference to his *crowning* glory, which was known to receive frequent ministrations from the local barber.

'Well, hurry it up then,' snapped Bronco. He snatched at the proffered glass and sank the entire contents in a single throw. He heaved a deep sigh of satisfaction, wiping the foam from his mouth. 'Wow! That sure hit the right spot!'

The King uttered a disdainful snort as if to say: didn't I tell you?

'Fill it up!' ordered Bronco, sliding the jug across the bar top. Weasel did so in a careless manner before mincing down to the far end of the bar to polish some glasses.

'You sure musta travelled some, feller,' surmised the shorter of the cowboys, giving the kid a full up-and-down.

Looking straight ahead, eyeballing the duo through the bar mirror, Bronco offered a brief reply.

'Bronco-bustin' on the Wind River. That's in Wyoming,' he added.

'I know where it is,' retorted the poke. A twisted leer bent the ugly puss out of line.

'Sure smells like it as well,' snorted the other, a large bulky jasper with a thick straggly moustache and greasy hair to match. He uttered a mirthless laugh, tweaking his nose with obvious meaning while purposefully shifting down the bar.

Bronco stiffened, his lips a tight, thin line, muscles coiled and sinewy.

At any other time he would have called these turkeys out. But in such situations, there was no telling how things might end up. Injury, broken bones, cuts and bruises – even a one-way trip to the mortuary.

He was no spineless weakling. On the frontier, a yellow streak marked a man for life, invariably following him around. Life for such people was pure misery, and they suffered worse than if they'd stood their ground in the first place. Constant insults regarding his own name had brought nothing but strife for George Coward. In the end, he had reverted to his mother's maiden name of Travis.

Struggling against all his instincts, Bronco swallowed his pride and backed off. He moved down the bar, picked up a pack of cards, and retired to a table at the rear of the saloon. He could positively feel the sneering contempt of the two cowpokes, their deriding looks stabbing him in the back. After finishing their pots, the duo left with a final salvo aimed specifically at the young man.

'Say, Big Jake, let's go find us a bar where real men do their drinkin',' spat the short, stocky fellow.

'You said it, Lefty,' responded the other with alacrity. 'I hate canaries, especially their colour.'

Bronco gripped the edges of the table. His teeth were grinding in frustration, the veins on his neck popping like wire cables.

Then the duo were gone.

Slowly he relaxed. Next time, he promised himself, that pair of beef jerkies wouldn't be so lucky. It didn't help to see that rancid bartender simpering to himself, clearly gloating in the kid's discomfort.

Bronco ignored him. Instead he concentrated on the inevitable visit from Flat Nose Jack Bowdrie. How would the bastard play it? It had been a log time, but he would never forget that face: a brand seared on to his memory for life.

He peered through the thick tobacco fog thrown up by the cardplayers. They hadn't even noticed the altercation. Drifting motes of dust were reflected by the sun beaming in through the front windows. Outside the hectic pace of life went on as usual. Inside the Bent Elbow, tension mounted. How long would he have to wait? Ten minutes, an hour?

The slam of the batwing doors shook him from his dreamy reverie. Two guys sauntered in. Seemingly undecided, they approached the bar slowly. Their backs were stooped with age and a lifetime's gruelling toil; Bronco recognized, from his erstwhile encounter with the miners, Nevada Jones and his wacky partner, Old Virginny.

The barweasel stumped up to them, a vexed grimace announcing his lack of patience with these particular customers.

'What do you pair of no-goods want?' he growled, the black curly moustache quivering with irritation.

'That ain't no way to speak to paying clients,' waxed Nevada Jones indignantly.

Virginny shook his head in agreement, blank eyes rolling.

'Show me the colour of your money. Then I'll serve you.'

'You know darned well we're waitin' on Bowdrie payin' us for the last poke he valued.' Nevada's gravelly voice rose an octave. 'And it's been nigh on three weeks since we handed it over.' He turned to his partner. 'Ain't that the case?'

Again, Virginny merely nodded. But his black eyes held those of the barkeep. Jim Finney wasn't nearly as half-baked as he liked folks to believe.

'*Mister* Bowdrie has a whole heap of claims to deal with,' the King rasped pompously. 'You'll just have to wait your turn. We don't give tick to miners.'

'And what are we expected to do in the meantime?' Nevada slammed a tight fist on the bar top.

'That ain't my affair,' said the King, moving away. 'Now clear off!' As far as he was concerned the matter was finished.

'Well I'm makin' it mine.'

The even tone, low-keyed and menacing, came from the back of the room.

'Give 'em anything they want.'

A silver dollar glinted in the flickering light of the oillamp as it flew across the room. It hit the polished mahogany of the bar and skittered across the shiny surface to land with a splash in the slops bucket.

Old Virginny cackled inanely. Jones peered through the gloom, not immediately recognizing his benefactor.

'Much obliged, mister,' he said.

Bronco rose and ambled across. The miners followed his easy gait with interest. He placed another five dollars on the bar.

'And keep 'em coming until that runs out.'

That's when the knowing arrived.

'Mr Travis!' Nevada's next words were aimed at his partner. 'See who it is, Virginny. It's Mr Travis.'

Finney nodded enthusiastically. 'I see him, Nevada. I see him.'

Smiles of gratitude and relief split their seamed faces.

'We'll have blue-label whiskey,' announced Jones haughtily, 'And make 'em doubles.'

Reluctantly, stifling an angry glower, King Arthur acquiesced.

'Could be we had you figured all wrong,' said Nevada addressing their benefactor. Then he lowered his voice. 'But you don't want to tangle with Bowdrie. He's real bad news.'

'Let me worry about that,' responded Bronco seriously. 'Now you fellers enjoy those drinks.'

'We won't forget this,' whispered Jim Finney. He caught the kid by the arm as Bronco turned to resume his seat and the unfinished game of solitaire.

Bronco shot him a quizzical frown.

It was an hour later.

Bowdrie had still not appeared. And the beerglass was empty. The two miners had left, assuring their new friend that repayment would be made with interest. Bronco smiled at the thought of the two old reprobates.

The moment passed.

Dispelling his wistful ruminations, the batwings swung open and a newcomer entered. One who instantly wiped the smile from his face: a Mexican, stout of girth and florid-faced with a thin pencil moustache. A cigarillo hung from thick rubbery lips. Close-set beady eyes, cold and calculating, scanned the interior. Only for the briefest of instants did they settle on the lone cardplayer before moving on.

Gomez.

Even after eight years, Bronco recognized one of his father's killers. The greasy smirk on the Mexican's round pudgy face held no trace of humour.

Bowdrie must reckon that only one man was needed to show this pipsqueak who was boss.

Slowly, without appearing to move, Bronco slipped his six-shooter from its holster and slid it beneath his hat. The butt, poking out from the rear, remained hidden from view. He dealt the cards for a new game, appearing not to notice the approaching Mexican. The chink of spurs ceased their jingling as Gomez stopped in front of the table. Still Bronco ignored him.

Gomez coughed. Only then did Bronco raise a single peeper.

He appraised the small man with a cool, almost insolent gaze.

'Something I can do for you, mister?' he purred.

Gomez removed the brown weed from his mouth and ground it underfoot.

'I theenk you know why I here, *señor*,' he said with a sing-song lilt.

'How's that?'

'The chestnut mare een Murphy's livery. Eet is your's, *sí?*'

'*Sí* is right,' returned Bronco, nonchalantly playing the Mex at his own game.

'But that is Meester Bowdrie's stall, *hombre*.' Gomez sounded almost apologetic, a ploy he often used to unsettle his opponents. It was usually the prelude to terminal gunplay. 'Hees own hoss no like any other stall. You understand, *señor*? And thee boss, he like hees hoss to be happy.' The Mex revealed a set of broken teeth. 'But, Meester Bowdrie, he no want trouble. So eef you agree to move it as I know you weel, he forget thee matter. Just a leetle mistake among friends, eh?'

Bronco casually lowered his eyes back to the cards.

The Mexican waited.

'Well, *señor*?' he asked eventually.

Bronco raised a thick eyebrow.

'You tell that flat-nosed critter that Bronco Travis decides where his horse will be liveried.' His tone had adopted a steely edge. 'And if'n he don't like it, tell him to send a proper man to pass the word.' He spat on the sawdust floor. 'Not some slimy greaseball.'

Gomez flushed a deep hue of purple. Nobody had ever spoken to him like that and lived to tell the tale. His eyes bulged. A guttural retort spluttered out in unintelligible Spanish. But the choice epithets needed no translation. Next he hunched down into the gunfighter's stance, right hand clawlike above the pearl-handled Schofield.

Other drinkers in the saloon immediately read the situation. Hurriedly they shifted out of the line of fire. King Arthur ducked down behind the bar.

Bronco's right hand rested on the butt of his pistol. Hawk-eyed, he watched the Mexican, studying the body language, waiting for that all-important sign that he was about to slap leather.

Time stood still, The two men faced each other, frozen like statues.

Then it happened: a slight lift of the right shoulder as Gomez went for his hogleg. Bronco instantly slammed his boot against the chair beneath the table, propelling it with gusto into the Mexican's legs. Thrown off balance, Gomez uttered a pained yelp. His shot went wide shattering the glass bowl of a hanging lantern.

Not so the shot loosed off by Bronco.

A .44 slug took a sizeable chunk out of the Mexican's left ear. His gun crashed to the floor as he grabbed for the injured appendage, blood pulsating through his fingers.

'Bastard!' he yelled, leaping about in wild disarray amidst the swirling blue of the gun smoke. The flailing antics resembled those of a circus clown. 'You pay for thees with your life, gringo.' The sing-song accent had been replaced by a whining tone. 'When I tell Meester Bowdrie, you dog meat, eh?' But the attempted threat had no teeth, and fell on deaf ears.

Bronco emitted a harsh laugh.

'I can't wait,' he spat, purposefully aiming the Frontier at the other appendage. 'Now git, else I'll be forced to even out that fat ugly mush.'

Gomez swallowed hard. He had no desire for a repeat performance. With a snarl, he turned and staggered out into the street. The saloon patrons slowly raised their heads, peering around, mouths agape.

'Sorry about the ruckus, folks,' said Bronco lightly. 'Some people just won't take no for an answer.' Then he stood up and ambled over to the bar, where he slammed a further heap of silver dollars down. 'The drinks are on me.'

That did it. Nobody needed a second bidding. There was a rush to take advantage of their good fortune. Free drinks were a rarity in Silverton. Suddenly the violent confrontation of a few minutes before was forgotten, just another incident added to the long list that had come to epitomize life in a boom town.

'Anybody know of a clean place to bed down for the night?'

Bronco's query was answered by one of the cardplayers.

'I can heartily recommended the Wyman Hotel across the other side of the street, friend. It's run by a fine upstanding lady by the name of Lily May Clanton.' The speaker paused in mid flow, his skull-like features soften-ing. 'Yes indeed, a mighty fine woman.'

Bronco turned with a hidden smirk. There was clearly more to this dude's association with the said Lily May than a mere good word as to her cooking ability.

Then he realized who had spoken — Foxy Dan Tanner, a right Jim Dandy. And a 'happily' married man, or had been. Tall and thin like a dressed-up skeleton, the black frock-coat, with nary a speck of dust in evidence matched the knife-edged creases in his slacks. A gold watch-chain and diamond stick-pin securing his silk necktie winked in the soft light. Surmounting the bony skull was a smart beige Stetson. Yet not even the wide brim could hide the devious gleam in the eyes. A sure giveaway that told of a man for whom double-dealing was second nature. Trust and honesty were alien to such beings.

Bronco's father had trusted this man.

'Miss Clanton usually has a room free,' continued Tanner effusively, thumbs tucked into his garish vest pock-ets. 'Just tell her that Mayor Tanner sent you.' He nodded as if acknowledging that the title would open any door in town.

So Foxy Dan was now mayor.

I wonder how many palms had to be greased for that to happen, wondered Bronco, while maintaining a bland expression of gratitude.

'Well, thank you, Mayor,' gushed Bronco with no attempt to conceal the hint of mockery. 'That's mighty hospitable of you.' As expected, the reply sailed over the other man's head. Tanner offered a glib smile before sink-ing his free drink and returning to the interrupted poker-game.

And not a flicker of recognition!

Bronco caressed his own drink. His mind began to wander, drifting back to another time, another age. Watery eyes fastened on to the amber nectar in his glass. Slowly they took on a glassy expression. The gently rising bubbles exerted a hypnotic force.

Hazy images began to appear. Slowly they sharpened into a nightmarish scenario.

THREE

IN THE BEGINNING

The year was 1869, the month May, the time 12.23 on a Saturday afternoon.

Henry Coward was sweeping the boardwalk outside his emporium. It was the only general store in the small settlement of Baker's Park. And Henry was about to close up for the day. Being a Saturday, many of the local ranchers had ridden in to replenish supplies. So business had been brisk.

It was also the day when retailers usually banked their takings. Henry usually wandered over to the Colorado Savings & National before lunch. He was looking forward to spending the rest of the day with his family. And following a leisurely meal prepared by Agnes, his wife of sixteen years, perhaps a buggy ride to meet up with his son.

George would most likely take the trail through Engineer Pass back from the Rocking-Chair Ranch, where he was buying a new horse, a chestnut mare sporting a white flash on its nose. He intended to call it Blaze. At full gallop, the animal had no equal. The impression of a rampant inferno fanning across the valley floor was a sight to behold.

Tomorrow was Sunday, the day of rest. After church, there was to be a picnic down-valley on the banks of the Animas. Life was indeed pleasant for Henry Coward, and the future looked decidedly rosy.

He turned his gaze to the west. The sky was a braided network of red and orange streaks melded to the azure backdrop.

That's when he noticed a haze of dust in the far distance. It emanated from a little-used side valley that led up to the old Crab Apple silver mine, long since abandoned. Nobody went up there now.

So who were these riders? And where had they come from?

Being the town marshal, if only part-time, Henry's curiosity was aroused. Apart from the odd drunk shooting at the moon, and the occasional dispute over land boundaries, nothing much ever happened to disturb the tranquil passage of time in Baker's Park.

Leaning on the broom handle, he watched as four horses detached themselves from the swirling yellow cloud. Five minutes later, the trail-weary riders entered the southern limits of the town and rode down Blair Street in line abreast. Half-closed eyes scanned the wooden false-fronted establishments on either side.

Passing in front of Henry's store, the gang hauled rein as if on cue. Closest to Henry, a tall, heavy-set rannie sporting a large black moustache aimed an icy glare at the storekeeper. His face was in shadow. A fragment of tumbleweed raced past down the street as if wishing to distance itself from the strange meeting.

That was when the man removed the high-crowned

Texan. Dark lank hair weaving through thick stubble coated his coarse features. Hard coal-black eyes held the storekeeper captive. Then the brutal visage split into a rabid grin, cold and merciless; all vestiges of humour had long since evaporated.

But it was the broken nose that punched Henry Coward back against the store front. His jaw dropped, a croak issuing from the dry throat.

Flat Nose Jack Bowdrie. Here in Baker's Park.

'Howdie, Marshal.' The tone was even, challenging. 'Said I'd be back, didn't I? Just like old times. And Jack Bowdrie always keeps his word.'

'Th – thought you was in the pen,' stammered Henry. 'The judge sent you down for a ten stretch.'

The gang all cackled at the idea.

'There ain't no jail can hold Jack Bowdrie for long. That right, boys?' The others nodded eagerly. 'And I got me some new *compadres*. Had to, didn't I, after my last partner got a taste of lead poisoning?' Bowdrie's face crinkled into a slough of abhorrence. 'But not before he left his calling-card, eh?'

Addressing the others, Bowdrie pointed a gloved paw at Henry's left arm.

'Show the boys the souvenir Hook left you with, Marshal.'

Henry ignored the offer. His arm had never been the same since. But at least he'd had the satisfaction of putting the slimy little toad into Boot Hill.

'That wouldn't be Hook Madigan would it, Jack?' enquired the ugly bruiser to his immediate left. Brick Stringer was broad as he was tall.

'Sure was,' responded Bowdrie shaking his head in mock regret. 'I'll miss the skinny critter . . . not to mention

33

his little friend, of course,' he added jokingly.

'How did he come by that hook, then?'

This from the third member of the gang – a square jawed young guy with chiselled good looks and an easy manner that belied a ruthless streak. Tom Gadds was clean-shaven, unlike the others who all sported various combinations of hirsute growth. He was always being ribbed about his fastidious nature when it came to personal hygiene, a trait that had earned him the nick-name of Pretty Boy — but only beyond earshot. A previous gang member had mistakenly scoffed openly at the handle; it had cost him dear.

'Lost his hand to a Ute brave in a knife fight. Over some squaw, would you believe,' jeered Bowdrie. 'The pesky Injun ran off claiming it as a prize.'

A blunt interruption cut short the ribald banter.

'You ain't wanted in this town, Bowdrie.'

Henry had at last found his voice. Summoning up his courage (sorely dented from the shock), and quelling the nausea in his guts, he continued: 'Just carry on riding, and don't stop.'

'You still here, Coward.' Bowdrie uttered a derisive snort, then purposely turned his back on the enemy. 'That's his name, boys. Coward by name, and coward by nature. Shot poor old Hooky in the back. Never gave him a chance.' Then slowly he swung round and faced down the marshal. 'You aimin' to do the same by me then . . . Coward?'

The rasping growl of this last insult brought an angry flush to Henry's cheeks. He stepped down on to the dusty street and grabbed the reins of Bowdrie's grey mare.

'I'm warning you, Bowdrie,' he threatened. 'If you haven't hit the trail by noon tomorrow, I'll—'

'You'll what?' scowled the gang boss, slapping at the storekeeper sardonically with his hat. 'Run me out of town with that broom?'

They all laughed heartily at Henry's discomfort.

'I'm theenking thees fellow needs a lesson een manners.'

The sing-song modulation of Gomez the Mexican was followed by the gang's manoeuvring their mounts around the hapless lawman. Kicked and spat on, Henry was jostled to the ground. He had the good sense to roll into a ball, thus avoiding injury from the stomping hoofs.

'That's enough, boys,' announced Bowdrie after what seemed an eternity, though actually little more than two minutes. 'Give the marshal some space. He needs time to sharpen up that broom, and maybe add a feather duster to his arsenal.'

Yipping and heehawing with gleeful abandon, the four hardcases drew their six-shooters and peppered the sign above Henry's store with bullet holes. Then they spurred off down the street in a wild gallop, dragging their sweating mounts to a steamy halt outside the Bent Elbow.

The shots had brought Agnes Coward rushing out on to the front porch. She uttered a startled gasp on seeing her husband staggering drunkenly in the middle of the street.

'Oh, Henry, what happened?' The wretched cry almost stuck in her throat. 'Who are those men?' Without waiting for an answer, she helped him back into the coolness of the store and sat him down on a chair. Always the practical one, Agnes slid round the counter and poured a generous measure of brandy into a glass.

'Drink this slowly,' she advised quietly, struggling to contain her anguish. 'It will calm you down. Then tell me why those men attacked you.'

While Henry sipped his drink and related the recent events, Agnes stroked his hair. Gently, she wiped the dust from his sweat-stained face. Henry was a good man, but he was no gunfighter. Ever since her husband had been persuaded, much against his better judgement, to accept the marshal's job, Agnes had lived in fear that something like this might happen.

Whenever she broached the subject about Bowdrie returning to avenge his incarceration in Denver's notorious penitentiary, Henry had always allayed her fears. The hatchet-faced polecat was safely locked up. And when released, he wouldn't dare return. The assurance had placated her, but only temporarily.

Now he was back. And burying that hatchet was not on the agenda, except in Henry's head if he wasn't careful.

The same thoughts were passing through Henry's mind. Unconsciously he gripped his wife's hand tightly, a shudder of dread rippling through his lean frame.

It was Henry's resolute sense of duty, a stoic resolve to do the right thing, that had driven his actions on that fateful day three years earlier.

Flat Nose Jack Bowdrie and his mean-eyed partner Hook Madigan had drifted into town and set themselves up in the Bent Elbow. They had rented a back room behind the saloon and spent much of the next few days lounging about with no apparent purpose in mind. Nobody paid them any attention.

It was only by pure chance that an old miner by the name of Stumpy Withers had taken a short cut to his own shack down the alleyway beside the saloon.

What he overheard through an open window stunned the old-timer to an abrupt halt. His hearing might not have been as acute as in his youth. But there was no mistaking the import of what the nefarious duo were planning.

Quick as his gammy leg would allow, Stumpy hobbled over to the general store where Henry Coward was cashing up.

Ever since he had prevented a shoot-out between two drunken cowhands, folks appeared to regard him as their benefactor, a sort of paladin. A persona he had not wanted, but had reluctantly accepted.

Hustling into the store, Stumpy could barely contain his disquiet.

'Take it easy, Stumpy,' advised a chuckling Henry Coward. 'Just calm down before you have a heart attack.'

The old guy sucked in lungfuls of oxygen before blurting out his momentous news.

'Cock an ear to this, Henry,' he spluttered grabbing at the counter for support. 'I just heard the darndest thing.'

Henry waited. Best to let Stumpy tell it in his own good time.

'Them two drifters, you know, the ugly cuss with a flat snout, and his hook-handed sidekick?'

Henry nodded, encouraging him to continue.

'Well, they only plan to rob the bank after closing hours today.'

Henry visibly stiffened. It being Saturday, he knew the bank vault would be overflowing. He also knew that Stumpy had an inventive imagination and often came up with bizarre fantasies to while away the hours. But surely he wouldn't conjure up something as serious as a robbery out of thin air.

'You sure about this?' He subjected the old guy to an intense stare.

Stumpy looked peeved. 'What yuh take me for, a story-teller?'

Henry raised an eyebrow but took the hint. His fore-head wrinkled in thought. Then he turned and lifted down a heavy twin-barrelled twelve-gauge from a shelf. He checked the load in both barrels, then moved round to exit the store.

'What yuh aiming to do, Henry?' enquired Stumpy, hopping around on his good leg.

'Get the drop on them before they try anything.'

'I'm comin' with you.' Stumpy drew his old Navy Colt.

'No you ain't,' ordered Henry.

There was no doubting the old miner's grit and deter-mination, but his days of hard-assing were long gone. Henry did not want the death of a friend on his conscience.

'Why in hell's name not?' wailed the slighted cripple.

' 'Cos I need you to alert the town council,' said Henry forcefully. 'Tell Dan Tanner to gather some men and cover that alley. I'll go in through the saloon and get the drop on them.'

Stumpy Withers snorted but realized that Henry's plan made sense. Then he left.

On hearing raised voices, Agnes had appeared from the back living-room.

'Why is it always you, Henry?' she pronounced with feel-ing. 'Why can't somebody else take responsibility for law and order in this town.'

'We ain't gotten no permanent law, honey,' he coun-tered.

'Well, it's about time Dan Tanner appointed some-body,' she snapped, vainly trying to pull her husband back from the open door. 'He's leader of the council.'

Henry gently shrugged her off. He knew where his duty lay. And so did Agnes. Secretly, she was proud that others saw fit to consult her husband when trouble loomed.

But a bank robbery. That was something else.

After giving Stumpy time to inform Tanner of the looming crisis, Henry slipped out through the door and strode purposefully across the street. Just as he was approaching the entrance to the alley the two robbers suddenly appeared. One was a heavy-set rannie. Over six feet in height, he sported a black *pistolero* type of moustache that concealed his lower lip. But it was the squashed and flattened nose, bent out of line, that drew the eye.

His partner gave the appearance of a dwarf in comparison. His claim to notoriety was the brass hook screwed into his right wrist.

Henry gave thanks that they were facing away from him. He was thus able to bring his gun to bear at shoulder-level and make the challenge.

'Hold it right where you are.' Henry thumbed back the hammers.

The warning rattle brought the two men to an abrupt halt. The brusque confrontation fastened them to the ground like statues.

'Now turn around and unhitch them gunbelts,' ordered Henry, his tone firm and uncompromising as he sidled closer. 'Make it slow and easy.'

'And who might you be?' snarled the big man, curling his lip.

'I'm the jasper who's arresting you.'

'On what charge?' shot back the big man.

'Attempted robbery.'

A stunned Bowdrie looked askance at his sidekick.

'How'd yuh figure that?'

'Got me a witness who heard you planning the whole caboodle,' replied Henry. 'Now drop them irons.'

'Reckon you got the balls to take us, then?'

Lacking the experience of dealing with hardened villains, Henry had stepped in too close. All his attention being fixed on the speaker, he failed to note the gleam in the dwarf s eye. Nor the flash of light as the lethal hook reached for his face. In the nick of time he was able to lift his arm to deflect the blow. But not before the razor-prong had gouged his arm down to the bone. Blood spurted from the lacerated limb in a fountain of red.

Henry yelled in agony.

Luckily he had the foresight to step back a pace. Through a pink mist of pain he saw the dwarf scuttling away down the alley. Without thinking, he raised the shotgun and loosed off both barrels. The last thing he saw before losing consciousness was a huge hole appearing in the man's back as he threw up his arms.

Only later did he learn that Stumpy Withers had kept Flat Nose covered with his old cap-and-ball until Dan Tanner chose to arrive with a deputation.

The prisoner was incarcerated in the tiny log cabin that served as a hoosegow until the circuit judge arrived. That was three weeks later. Conducted by Judge Tyrone (known by all and sundry as Cold Heart Tyrone due to his penchant for full-term sentencing), the result of the trial was a foregone conclusion. Bowdrie was given ten years in the state penitentiary. Threats of retribution made by the outlaw were laughed off. Empty words with no substance.

After the trial, life in Baker's Park once again reverted to normality. And everybody thought that that was the last they would ever see of Flat Nose Jack Bowdrie.

FOUR

THE WHIP HAND

Now he was back, intent on revenge, and with three hard-nosed gunslingers to back him up. Although the judge had sent him down with the town's backing, Henry knew it was a personal vendetta. Bowdrie held him responsible for his incarceration.

At that moment, the shop door flew open. A man dressed in range garb stepped into the cool interior. Sunset Johnson ran a small chicken farm in the Gila Bend valley up around the Red Mountain. He supplied Henry with fresh eggs and meat. Nobody knew his real name, nor the origin of the lurid scalp blemish from which his nick name came. A small, friendly guy in his early forties, Sunset was a family man who had never been known to wear a gun.

Until now.

The heavy Dragoon revolver tucked into his leather belt looked out of place.

'I heard that Bowdrie's back,' he gasped out, 'Him and his gang are down at the Bent Elbow getting all liquored up. Stumpy Withers was in there. Claims that Bowdrie's been a-braggin' how he broke out of the pen.' Sunset paused to draw breath before resuming his flow, 'And how he reckon it's is payback time, marshal.'

'I already had words with him,' pronounced Henry.

'Yeah? Well, if you want help, you only gotta ask. I'll back you to the limit.' Sunset patted the rusty old pistol. 'When that scumbag finds the whole town's agin him, he'll have to back down. We'll show him who's in charge.'

'Much obliged for your support,' said Henry, giving the pistol a wry smile. 'I'll let you know the score when I've spoken to the town council.'

'Don't you forget, Marshal,' pressed Johnson with fervour. 'Soon as you've gathered a deputation together, just let me know.'

'I surely will, Sunset.'

The chicken farmer nodded, then left.

Next to arrive was Stumpy Withers, who likewise offered his help. Henry sent the old-timer off to find Dan Tanner to summon a meeting of the town council.

All he could do now was wait. The afternoon dragged on.

Henry tried to keep himself occupied in the store. But his thoughts kept tumbling back to Bowdrie's supposedly empty threats. He certainly hadn't returned merely to humiliate him in a street ruckus. The support of friends and customers would be much appreciated, that was for sure. Bowdrie and his gang couldn't buck the whole town. They'd be forced to back off.

Henry twiddled his thumbs until well after sundown. Still no sign of Tanner.

'Where are they?'

The taut enquiry to his wife went unanswered. He went out on to the boardwalk in front of the store and surveyed the street. Empty. Not even a dog cocking its leg. On Saturday night, Blair Street was always busy. It seemed that the whole town had learned of Bowdrie's return and were keeping well out of the way.

Henry's jaw tightened. An anxious frown troubled his features.

'I'm going to see Tanner,' he announced firmly before nervously running a hand through his hair. 'He must have arranged a deputation by now.'

'You think so?' Agnes was sceptical. 'They're scared, Henry. Frightened to challenge a bunch of tough gunmen like those Bowdrie's gathered together. Best accept the fact that nobody's about to stick their necks out to save yours.'

'Sunset Johnson offered to help,' Henry muttered with little conviction.

Agnes gave a derisive grunt that said it all.

'A chicken farmer who has only ever shot at rabbits?'

She grabbed her husband roughly by the shoulder and turned him face on. The classical beauty that had so enchanted Henry Coward was set immutably like a slab of cold marble. Desperately, she tried to keep the panic from her voice as she pleaded with him to leave Baker's Park.

Henry listened. But his mind was a confusion of chaotic thoughts. His wife's entreaty left him haunted by the vision of a dire future forever looking over his shoulder.

'When?' he asked in a low voice. His face had assumed the grey pallor of death.

'Soon as George returns. I can have the wagon loaded within the hour.'

'But where will we go?' he questioned, desperately searching for some other solution to this impossible dilemma.

'My sister's place in Durango. She has a couple of spare rooms. And it would give us some breathing space.' Her pleading eyes were glued to the tormented figure of the man she loved above all else, silently begging for his compliance.

Henry rose to his feet and paced up and down the store. His trembling brow was knitted into a mesh of perplexity. What should he do?

Take the easy way out? After all, didn't he have a responsibility to his family? They could just ride away. Forget about Baker's Park and start a new life elsewhere.

But what about his duty? Not only to the town, but to himself. What price his self-respect? If he ran now, that would be it. To all and sundry, Henry Coward would be just that. The man with the yellow streak. The spineless wimp who ran away. He would be shunned and derided by all, for the rest of his life. Could he live with that?

Henry paused in mid-stride. His wife held her breath, green eyes wide, staring, nerves at fever-pitch. Waiting, studying her husband's every move.

No!

Henry's back straightened. A rush of adrenalin pumped through his tight frame. Head held high, he walked to the rear of the store and tugged open a drawer beneath the counter.

She knew at that moment that her pleas had fallen on deaf ears. Her shoulders slumped. There was nothing more to be said. Henry had made up his mind. And nothing she could say would change that.

He pulled up a stool and broke down the Remington New Model Army pistol. He methodically began to clean and oil each working part. The weapon had been newly issued to the Northern forces during the Civil War in 1863 as a percussion revolver, Henry had had his converted to cartridge once the conflict had ended. He had not fired it in anger for six months. And that was only a couple of warning shots over the heads of a dozen cowboys from rival outfits involved in a fist fight.

The evening meal was consumed in virtual silence and young George couldn't help but pick up on the brittle atmosphere. Henry allayed his son's disquiet, forcing himself to take an interest in the boy's new chestnut mare as he enthused with excitement about how he'd pushed the animal to full gallop.

Henry barely slept a wink that night. And the light of dawn arrived all too soon.

The day of reckoning.

Not wishing to break with routine, he insisted that Agnes and the boy attend the Sunday morning service as usual. George ran on ahead to meet some friends. Agnes tried desperately to remain calm – for Henry's sake. When at last she left the store, a tender kiss, a gentle touch of hands and a backward look testified both to the pride and to the deepest anxiety each felt for the other.

What the next hour would bring, only the Lord God could determine. Henry sat down, uncorked a bottle of Blue Label hidden under the store counter, and took a hefty slug. Several slugs later, he flipped open his pocket-watch. It read fifteen minutes after noon.

Purposefully the part-time marshal of Baker's Park donned the old army gunbelt with its shiny accessory. Tightly clutching the Loomis shotgun to his chest, he stepped outside on to the boardwalk and paused, uneasily peering up and down the street. It was still deserted. Not even Sunset Johnson had shown up. Probably he was in church with the others a-praying for their souls.

Henry had secretly entertained a vague aspiration that Blair Street would be filled with armed men eager and willing to support their part-time law officer. It had been a futile hope. A day-dream.

Then.

From around the corner, the stooped figure of Stumpy Withers appeared. He was clutching an old Sharps hunting rifle.

'All set then, Marshal,' he asserted confidently. It was clear that the cripple had harboured a similar expectation. 'Where is everyone?'

Henry gave him a doubtful smile, then nodded towards the newly painted white chapel. The building gleamed in the sunlight.

'Go home. Stumpy,' he said in a flat monotone. 'This is between me and Bowdrie now.'

'But I wanna help,' implored the old guy.

'No sense in you gettin' shot up for no reason.' A warm smile of gratitude parted the lawman's ashen lips. 'Much obliged, Stumpy,' he said. 'Now go on home.'

Leaving the old man with a bemused expression playing over his gnarled visage, Henry gingerly stepped down and slowly walked towards the Bent Elbow, some four blocks north. Leaden feet trailed in the dust. The hiss of wind filtering through the clapboard frontages sounded a portent of doom.

At the far end of the street, a faint hum came to his ears - the light cadences of distant singing. A lone buzzard perched on the chapel spire, taciturn and watchful.

While still some two blocks from the saloon, Henry sensed rather than saw movement to his right and left. Flitting shadows. He stopped. That was when they surrounded him.

Jack Bowdrie was in front, flanked by the Mexican, known only as Gomez. The gang leader hadn't even bothered to draw his gun, such was his arrogant disdain for the man who had sent him down. Thumbs hooked arrogantly into his twin-holstered gunbelt, Bowdrie speared the lawman with a baleful glower.

Henry backed up a pace. But the metallic click of a cocked Navy Colt stayed his retreat. Behind, Tom Gadds, the 'pretty boy', offered a leery smirk. To his left, the big man, Brick Stringer, drew heavily on a cigar. Blue smoke twisted suggestively from thick rubbery lips. Casually, Stringer flicked the smouldering butt away.

It was Bowdrie who broke the silence.

Not by any mere utterance.

The time for words was long gone. A sharp crack split the air as a twelve-foot length of plaited hide snaked out towards its prey. As it coiled around the barrel of the Loomis, the gun was jerked from Henry's grasp and flicked across the street beyond his reach, now a mere chunk of useless metal. Another swirl of cowhide enfolded his body in its raw embrace, sending him effortlessly gyrating like a child's top.

Suddenly Henry was at the mercy of four bullwhips.

Long brown tentacles flashed through the air thudding into the writhing figure. He opened his mouth – only a choking retch issued forth. Desperately, he tried to thwart the biting serpents. But to no avail. His blue shirt was soon torn to shreds.

Yarraping and baying like demented fiends, the hardcases continued their brutal assault with a vengeanc. Saliva dribbled obscenely from mouths contorted with the lust for blood. All traces of humanity had deserted them as a baser, more earthy instinct took control. This was the law of the wild, wolves scenting the ultimate kill.

Henry slumped to the ground, unable to defend himself. Blood welled from a myriad lacerations transforming the ragged blue shirt into the colour of hellfire. Nor were these men slouches when it came to handling the bullwhip. Their aim concentrated on the upper body with a deadly accuracy born of frequent usage. Henry's face was soon just a lump of raw meat. He was barely recognizable as the handsome, upstanding town marshal.

But the infernal clamour had attracted an audience.

At the north end of Blair, the chapel doors swung open as the good citizens of Baker's Park tentatively emerged, to discover the gruesome scene they had all hoped to avert. As they milled about in confusion like nervous sheep, fear laced with a liberal helping of guilt was written on every face.

Persuasion from the town council led by Dan Tanner had readily placed the responsibility for dealing with this current threat squarely on to the shoulders of the law. And it was Henry Coward who wore the tin star. An emblem of position, of prestige and respectability. After all, wasn't he paid to uphold the law? And wasn't it he whom Jack Bowdrie was really after? Surely all that was needed were strong words and a firm hand to force the gang into leaving town, tails between their legs.

Such a naïve assumption had been a figment of pure fantasy.

Any contrite thoughts were cut short by a new sound slicing through the tense atmosphere. Crushing in its ferocity, the gut-wrenching howl of anguish instantly silenced the anxious mutterings.

For a full minute George Coward stood glued to the chapel steps, frozen into immobility, his face a mask of horror. All eyes turned towards him. Then like the parting of the Red Sea, the crowd separated.

Another pained holler burst from deep within as he dashed through the gap and up the street. Tall and gangly, the fourteen-year-old boy frantically waved his arms, screaming at the gang to stop the beating.

'Bastards!' he cursed, ploughing into the big man with a black moustache who was clearly the leader. 'What have you done to my father? Leave him be.' Thin arms pummelled at the gang boss. Bowdrie effortlessly warded off the puny blows. An evil grin cracked the flinty exterior.

'Ornery cuss, ain't he?'

The others hooted with derision.

Suddenly. Bowdrie's sardonic smile vanished. Losing interest in the uneven contest, he uttered a manic growl. Then he grabbed the boy with his left hand while delivering a stunning blow to the jaw with his right. The force spun George in a tight circle. He crashed to the ground, blood pumping from a split lip.

His groggy eyes eventually focused to meet those of his father.

'Noooooooo!' he howled, lunging for the discarded shotgun.

The gang were taken by surprise; it was Brick Stringer who recovered first. Though large and cumbersome, he could move swiftly when the occasion demanded. Three rapid steps and his boot slammed the weapon from the boy's grasp, the wooden stock cracking against his forehead.

Always the faithful henchman, Stringer looked to Bowdrie for instructions.

'What should I do now, boss?' came the slow drawl.

Before he could respond, Agnes Coward elbowed past

the hulking bruiser and slumped to her knees beside her injured son.

'Let him alone. He's only a boy.' Maternal instinct surged to the fore.

'Well now,' smirked Bowdrie, ogling the comely female with a lascivious leer. 'Seems as how the kid has a champion. I could do with some of that and no mistake.' The lewd implication was plain.

Sniggers all round. For the moment, Henry Coward was forgotten.

'Hold fast there, Jack,' butted in Tom Gadds with mock admonishment. 'Ain't that sort of thing more in my line?' The pretty boy flicked back his long blond hair with a flourish.

Agnes hugged her son protectively, scrabbling crablike away from the bawdy comments.

'You keep away,' she snapped forcefully, though her tone had a tremulous edge. Tears trickling down her smooth cheeks were of frustration and anger rather than fear. 'Does it have to take four gutless lowlifes to handle a defenceless woman?' Following this furious invective, she spat at their feet.

Bowdrie snarled. His coarse features hardened. Nobody spoke to him like that. Not even a woman. He raised his hand in warning.

All the gang's attention had been focused on the woman and her son. The lull had given Henry a welcome respite. He thanked providence that the gang had failed to relieve him of the Remington. Through pulsating waves of pain, he sensed that this was his last chance to turn the tables. He drew the revolver and thumbed back the hammer. His vision blurred.

Far away in another world a dog barked. A store sign

offered a fateful squeak. Windows rattled out a stutter of impending tragedy. And the gun barrel swung in a tired arc. In slow motion.

Too slow!

Gomez had perceived the surreptitious stirring.

In the flick of a rattler's tongue, he whipped out his shooter and blasted off three quick shots. Each found its mark. The lawdog slammed backwards. But not before his twitching muscles loosed off a response. The slug clipped Bowdrie's boot-heels almost upending the gang leader.

Four pairs of eyes, malevolent and cruel, switched to the dying marshal. A baying shriek of rage sprang from Bowdrie's throat.

'Show that son-of-a-bitch the *Denver Sieve*,' he hollered. As one, the quartet drew their pistols and emptied them into the jerking torso.

Agnes Coward screamed, the heaving lamentation merging with the hollow echo of death. She buried her face in her son's shoulder. As he began to recover from Stringer's savage kick, a hideous scenario assailed the boy's ragged senses. It was a scene that would haunt George Coward for years to come. Many times he would awake soaked with sweat as the nightmare once again asserted itself.

The boy's blood-caked face set in a grim mask of hate. Eyes narrowed to thin slits, dark impenetrable caverns, as he silently made his own pledge of vengeance. These animals would rue the day they came to Baker's Park. Daggers of loathing stabbed the backs of the four desperadoes as they walked away. Laughing and joking, they strolled down the middle of the street as if they owned it. A job well done.

Left behind, a bleeding corpse. Now forgotten.

But not by George Coward!

Slowly Agnes rose to her feet. She poked an accusing finger at the huddling mass of humanity outside the chapel. Her words, carefully expressed, were damning in their condemnation.

'Call yourselves our friends. You abandoned Henry when he needed you the most?' The contempt in her voice was unmistakable. 'Scared rabbits, that's what you are, hiding away in God's house. These gunslingers may have pulled the trigger, but you are as much to blame. And I want nothing more to do with you or your miserable town.'

The good citizens of Baker's Park shuffled uncomfortably stung by the scathing denunciation. The truth hurt.

Suddenly a single shot rang out. It came from behind the general store.

Later, the body of Stumpy Withers would be found, the back of his head smeared against the wall. Poking from his open mouth was the barrel of a Sharps hunting rifle.

FIVE

LILY MAY CLANTON

'So you're still here.'

Bronco nodded to himself sinking the last mouthful of beer. His taut comment referred to Jack Bowdrie.

'Sure I'm here, mister,' responded a figure to his left, pushing a mop around the plank floor. 'Every day and every night. That's me. Sunset Johnson at your service.'

Bronco gave the swamp dog a puzzled look, then the realization dawned. The old jasper thought he was talking to him.

'Sunset?' queried Bronco with a lazy smile.

Yes, he remembered now. The chicken farmer. He appeared to have come down in the world.

Johnson removed his tattered hat to reveal a large vivid scar. Ragged at the edges, it was a macabre blend of reds and purples with an orange blot the size of a dollar piece taking centre stage.

'Apaches disapproved of my gold prospectin' down New Mexico way,' he commented wryly. 'Gave me a close haircut for free.' Sunset rubbed the blemish before resuming his mopping around Bronco's chair. 'Damn blasted savages left me for dead. And I would have been but for a Good Samaritan what found me on the trail near Tucson.' Jackson paused for effect. 'None other than Wild Bill Longley!' he warbled, bobbing his head like a hungry bald eagle.

The old-timer waited for the expected reaction. He wasn't to be disappointed. The story had earned him a heap of extra drinks in the past.

'Longley, you say?' Bronco pursed his lips and blew a low whistle. He certainly knew of the Texas gunfighter, if only by reputation. 'Now that is one bad dude to tangle with.'

'Treated me like I was kin,' continued Jackson, leaning on his mop. 'Paid for me a hotel in Tucson, and the best sawbones to sew me up.'

Jackson licked his lips expectantly. Bronco split a wide grin. He knew the score. Slowly he extracted a silver dollar from his vest pocket and flipped it into the air. Quick as a flash a gnarled hand shot out and grabbed the spinning coin.

'Much obliged, young feller. Anything you need to know about Silverton, just ask old Sunset Johnson.' The swamper was already heading for the bar, his eyes glazed over in feverish anticipation of the drinks to come.

'I'll remember that.' Bronco smiled at the old guy's swiftly retreating back.

Then his gaze clouded over. Uneasy thoughts assailed his mind as to the means his revenge on Flat Nose Bowdrie would take. But first he needed a meal and a bed for the night. Foxy Tanner had suggested the Wyman Hotel. He knew it well, although a new owner appeared to have taken charge.

A perplexed expression creased the young man's visage as he made for the saloon door. It seemed that a good many of the town's previous residents had upped stakes and left during the intervening years. Was that because of a guilty association with the murder to which they had been party? Or had Bowdrie driven them out? He shook his head. Perhaps he would never know.

What mattered now was keeping one step ahead of the bastard, and keeping his eyes peeled for trouble. Bronco had every confidence in his ability to take out the gang boss. And he was eager to meet him face to face.

Passing the end of the long bar, he drew level with Sunset Johnson.

'Tell me, old man,' he murmured in a low voice. 'Where does Jack Bowdrie hang out?'

Jackson peered at him over the rim of his glass. His eyes widened. Fear stalked unfettered behind the brown orbs. Unsteadily he grabbed hold of Bronco's arm.

'You keep away from that treacherous sidewinder, mister,' he warned, nudging him further down the bar out of earshot. His voice was slurred from the booze, but the nuance was unambiguous. 'Bowdrie is one nasty critter. You cross him, he'll cut out your liver and feed it back to you piece by piece. He's done it afore. And sure as eggs is eggs, he'll do it again.'

With a brief nod the swamper returned to a more pressing need. Nobody, it appeared, had a good word for Flat Nose Jack Bowdrie. And Bronco still had no idea where his hangout was.

Bronco shrugged and headed down the street for the Wyman Hotel. Luckily it was on the same side. No need to get his boots all dirtied up. As he entered the restaurant he noticed that only a couple of tables were occupied. He chose one against the back wall facing the door. He had no intention of being bushwhacked from behind.

A large woman of around forty years was sitting behind a counter. With some effort she lifted her frame off a high-backed chair and sashayed across the room. Gliding between tables laid with green-and-white checked cloths, she displayed a surprisingly nimbleness for a woman of substance.

Her heavily rouged mouth broke into a wide smile of welcome. Light from the crystal chandelier specially imported from Denver emphasized the gleaming white of her teeth.

This had to be Lily May Clanton. A voluminous green dress matched the bouffant hair piled high like a wedding cake and finished off with a green silk ribbon. Swaying in time to the measured tread, the ample bosom drew the eye like a moth to a flame. Even Bronco had to persuade his bulging peepers to rise above the deep cleavage.

Lily May was well aware of her effect on male patrons and blatantly exploited her indisputable assets. Here was a woman who had seen it all. Each crease around the eyes spoke of a life where extremes of joy and sadness went hand in hand. Bronco now understood Foxy Dan Tanner's impious intentions towards this 'fine lady'. He idly wondered if the feelings had been reciprocated.

'What'll it be then, mister'?' she asked, giving the young man the once-over. A twinkle in her bright blue eyes indicated that she liked what she saw. Even beneath the dark stubble and trail dust, Bronco Travis was himself a fine-looking young man.

He cast an eye towards the chalkboard advertising the day's fare.

'What do you recommend?' he asked.

The woman threw him a reproving glance. Hands on ample hips, she replied:

'If I was to say the steak pie, then that would mean I didn't rate the beef stew too highly. And what would that mean?'

She waited for a reaction, plucked eyebrows raised.

'Well?'

Bronco looked suitably puzzled.

'What it would mean,' she said slowly as if to a child, 'is that I'd be left with a pot full of stew that would end up in the pig swill. Not a particularly good way to run a business, wouldn't you say?' She leaned over him, revealing more than the gold pendant round her neck.

The young man swallowed and offered a conciliatory nod.

'So I'll leave it in your capable hands to make that mind-boggling decision.' A mischievous smirk beamed from the painted face. 'Beef stew or steak pie?'

'Uhmmmm!' murmured Bronco playing along. 'That sure is a difficult one.' He stroked his rough chin, the dark eyes creasing at the edges. 'Beef stew or steak pie,' he repeated slowly.

Lily May sighed knowing he was teasing her, but enjoying the game nonetheless.

'Make it beef stew,' he said at last. The proprietor smiled with a bobbed curtsey, then turned towards the kitchen. 'And some extra dumplings would slide down a treat,' he added nonchalantly.

Lily May kept walking but gave him an unmistakably rude gesture behind her back. Bronco chuckled but knew the extras would be delivered. He shook his head. Whoever married such a feisty lady would indeed be a brave soul. But there was no denying that he would be well fed. Maybe the cooking offered by Foxy Tanner's wife, Elizabeth, was more akin to that enjoyed by cowboys on a trail drive. Bronco couldn't resist a hearty guffaw.

When the food arrived, he tucked in with gusto.

'The chow up to your expectations then, mister?'

'Ain't tasted better since I left home.'

Bronco wiped the gravy from his mouth with a green napkin. The allusion to home brought a tightening of the jaw. The roguish eyes dimmed as more painful recollections surged to the fore, a reminder of his 'unfinished business' here in Silverton.

It had been three years since George Coward had left home – if you could call it that. Following his father's murder, the family had moved to Durango. His Aunt Daisy had tried her best, but mother and son living in one room above a bakery was no life for either of them.

So when Cyrus Grant, a local freight haulier, had shown more than a passing interest in the bereaved widow, the outcome was a foregone conclusion. Transporting silver from local mining settlements into Durango had made Cyrus a wealthy man. And he owned a large house on a hill overlooking the town.

It was an ideal place for a young boy to grow up and consign his nightmares to the past where they belonged. George would now be able to continue his education in Durango's prestigious academy and make something worthwhile of his life.

His new stepfather assured the boy and his mother that everything would be done to bring the perpetrators of the heinous crime to justice. Months passed and nothing further was heard. Excuses piled up. The sheriff was doing his best. Proof of guilt was hard to gather. Nobody was willing to give evidence.

Not only that: the dream of a new life soon turned sour. Far from being the philanthropic saviour he had affected to be, Cyrus Grant had proved to be a callous brute, and a frequent visitor to the notorious Strutting Peacock — a house of ill-repute.

And George never saw the inside of the academy. He was put straight to work unloading the wagons and cleaning the stables. Forced to labour from dawn 'til dusk for a pittance, the hard drudgery was little short of slave labour.

He suffered in silence, even though very early on he came to loathe his stepfather. He worked hard, mainly to please his mother, who, he assumed, was happy with the arrangement. What he did not know was that Agnes Coward (now Grant) was suffering an equal amount of anguish. The marriage was a sham. All Cyrus wanted was an unpaid skivvy to do his bidding, both as housekeeper and bedmate.

When she refused him what he considered to be his conjugal rights, violence erupted. On numerous occasions George had wondered why his mother stayed in her room for days at a time, or wore tinted spectacles. Heavy make-up covered the more obvious bruises.

But she always adopted an air of grace and dignity in his presence. Agnes knew that divorce was out of the question. Such women were ostracized from society, became outcasts who often ended their days in places like the Strutting Peacock. Whenever the notion came into her mind, it was quickly discarded. She persuaded herself that life was at least tolerable. As the wife of one of Durango's leading citizens, she commanded respect and led a relatively comfortable existence. But none of this opulent lifestyle was true compensation for what she and her son had lost.

She entertained hopes that one day George would inherit the haulage business. Such dreams kept her going through the dark lonely nights when Cyrus ranted and raved after one of his drinking sprees.

Due in no small measure to his mother's persuasion when her husband was in one of his more co-operative moods, George was allowed to keep his beloved chestnut mare, although Grant insisted the boy pay for the animal's upkeep out of his own meagre wages.

Another prized possession, kept well hidden, was a Navy Colt bought from a miner who was upgrading to a Starr double-action revolver. For an extra two dollars the guy had thrown in an army holster and shell-belt. George cut off the button-down flap and rubbed bear grease into the tough leather to make it supple. With a sharp knife he carefully etched his initials into the rosewood grip.

Practising in secret, he soon became a crack shot and no sluggard when it came to the fast draw. At every opportunity on his day off he would venture into the canyons beyond the confines of Durango, hunting mainly rabbits and small game.

And with expertise came a new-found confidence, a swaggering gait, tinged with a hint of youthful recklessness. By the age of eighteen, George had taken to wearing the well-oiled rig openly. It would only be a matter of time before the simmering pot boiled over.

In fact, it was almost five years since he and his mother had first come to live in Durango.

One day, as he returned early to the house he had grudgingly come to call his home, George's mind was on the Saturday dance in town. He had his eye on a certain young seamstress and needed the extra time to make himself presentable.

The sight he beheld on entering the front door was the final proof of all that he had suspected. Grant had his big hands entwined in his mother's hair and was shaking her like a ragdoll. A livid purple bruise on her cheek testified to the beating she had already endured. His other hand was poised to deliver another stunning blow.

Neither had noticed George's silent entry. Over the years, entering quietly had become a habit, principally to avoid meeting the callous brute and the sarcastic comments that inevitably followed.

He stood in the entrance to the main hallway, rooted to the spot, so great was the shock of seeing his mother being violated by this drunken bully.

'Don't lie to me!' snarled Grant, his blotchy face contorted in a drunken frenzy of rage. 'You arranged to meet that snivelling wretch while my back was turned.'

'No Cyrus, I'm telling you,' cried the cowering woman, 'He was only here to measure up for the wallpaper.'

A caricature of a laugh spewed forth as Grant continued his tirade.

'Don't give me that,' he ranted. 'You're nothing but a cheap whore.'

A sharp crack broke the mesmerizing spell as Agnes Grant screamed. She fell back, blood streaming from a cut lip.

That was when George reacted.

'Take your filthy hands off my mother.'

The boy's measured yet tremulous utterance sliced through the venomous atmosphere. Grant swung to face the intruder. His teeth were bared in a rabid leer.

'What you doing here?'

'Seems like I arrived just in time.' George had recovered his composure. His gaze was bleak and steady, fists clenched in tight balls. 'You're nothing but a stinking wife-beater, a yellow rat that needs stamping on.'

Grant's bloated features twisted into an irate glare. Then he moved over to a bureau, opened a drawer and removed a whip.

'You need a lesson in manners, boy.' The thin smile on his gaunt features held not a trace of humour. 'I've been too lenient with you. Let you have too much of your own way. A taste of this will teach you some respect for your betters.' He shook out the writhing serpent.

Again Agnes screamed, then flung herself at the brute whom she had once mistakenly thought would protect her and George. He easily pushed her away, then raised the pitiless scourge. George felt he was being suffocated by a red cloying mist. The blood rushed to his head. All the pent-up frustrations of years under this tyrant's brutal power surged to the fore. And the swaying whip brought the memories flooding back with the force of a tidal wave.

A roar of anger burst from his throat. And before he knew it, the gun was in his hand belching flame. Three times the ancient Colt spat lead, each slug finding its mark in the chest of Cyrus Grant. He staggered back under the impact, a hazy apparition lost in the black powder-smoke issuing from the barrel. Muscles contracting, the hulking brute crashed into a deal table. He was dead before he hit the floor.

A palpable silence enfolded the grim scene. Both mother and son were unable to accept the awful truth of what had taken place. George was shaking uncontrollably. This was not the same as shooting at rabbits. His gun fell to the wooden floor.

The harsh echo jerked Agnes back to the reality of their situation. What to do now?

Pragmatic and methodical, she led her son into the kitchen and poured him a tot of brandy. Unused to the fiery spirit, George coughed and spluttered as it burnt a path down his throat. But it had the desired effect.

Initially, Agnes considered the best way out of this mess was to claim the shooting was an accident. Cyrus had been cleaning his gun while under the influence.

This notion was shattered by a scream emanating from the hall. Rose, the housemaid, had become used to raised voices in the Grant household. But gunfire inside the house was something different. It was the staccato burst that had brought her running down the stairs from her garret at the top of the house. There she discovered the master's dead body with young Mr Coward's smoking gun beside it.

Not waiting for any explanations, the girl ran outside yelling to anybody within earshot:

'Quick! Quick! Get the marshal. There's been a shooting. Mr Grant has been murdered.'

That altered things entirely.

Within the hour, Blaze was saddled and George Coward was leading a pack-mule out across the back lot heading south away from Durango. The last time he saw his mother alive, her hand was raised. The normally bright eyes were puffy and bloodshot, her proud shoulders stooped. He had let her down badly.

He turned away, tears coursing down sunken cheeks. The endless drift of broken mesa country stretched away to the horizon. Spiny grama grass and yucca pockmarked the arid terrain. A yawning pit of despair filled the aching void in his stomach. The future looked bleak. And as if to compound the hurt, dark clouds brushed the surrounding peaks of the San Juan Mountains. Heavy drops of rain soon followed. In no time, he was drenched to the skin.

He patted the chestnut mare's neck, receiving a brief snort of acknowledgement. At least he had one friend. There was no turning back now. Next stop New Mexico, where he could disappear amidst the desert canyons and start a new life.

'So what's wrong with the stew?'

Bronco gazed steadily into the brown mixture, a fork in one hand and a hunk of bread in the other. Neither had moved for two minutes.

A nudge in the back brought the young man out of his wistful preoccupation.

'Didn't quite catch that, ma'am,' he mumbled forking a chunk of beef into his mouth.

'I figured you had something against my cooking,' responded Lily May Clanton, 'Seeing as how you wasn't eating.'

'Just thinkin'. That's all.'

'Anything in particular?'

'You could say.' He didn't elaborate. How could he?

Cyrus Grant wasn't the only rannie to get on the wrong side of his gun hand. There had been three others. And each time, the killing had become easier. Death rides easy when you have nothing to lose. Not that he enjoyed spilling human blood. He was able to justify each death. At least he figured his conscience was clear. The dead men had earned their passage to hell.

And he had no doubts that more would follow. A rough grinding of teeth as he chewed on the meat was all that betrayed pent-up inner turmoil. That and a waxy grey pallor that hinted at numerous sleepless nights.

Lily May moderated her tone.

'Didn't mean to pry,' she said recognizing that this

stranger had a past he had no wish to share. A history best left untold. She moved away, leaving the young man to finish his meal.

After his coffee and a well-earned cigar, Bronco paid the bill.

'Best stew I've tasted in six months,' he avowed, setting his hat straight and slinging the dual saddle pack across his left shoulder. Lily May smiled.

'Glad you enjoy it, mister,' she replied.

'Heard tell that you might have a room to let.'

'Could be,' came back the quick response. 'How long would you be staying in Silverton?'

He shrugged. 'Hard to say. One week, maybe two.'

She reached behind and unhooked a key.

'Number three. Up the stairs then along the corridor to the end.'

'Much obliged, ma'am,' said Bronco tipping his hat. Turning to leave, he paused. 'You wouldn't happen to be a friend of Foxy Dan Tanner would you?' he added.

Lily May speared him with a curious look.

'You know Foxy then?'

'We've met.'

She tried to read behind the steady gaze, but the grey eyes remained inscrutable, steady and impassive. And how did this stranger know about Dan Tanner's nickname? The mystery surrounding the young man intensified with each passing minute.

The suggestion of a smile lit up her face. She chose her reply carefully, matching the young man's enigmatic gaze.

'He would like to be more friendly than I'm prepared to allow.'

'And what about Jack Bowdrie?'

'Keep clear of that son-of-a-bitch.' Lily May's vigorous

curse took Bronco by surprise. His thick eyebrows lifted.

'Everybody in this town has been giving me the same advice,' he said.

'And you'd do well to take it. That critter is bad news.'

Bronco offered a thoughtful nod of acknowledgement, then turned without another word and went up to his room.

SIX

ONE CLOSE SHAVE

It was pitch black. Suddenly he was surrounded by a dozen flaming brands. They were held by faceless men, ghosts from the past, who just stood there in silence, waiting. A light breeze fanned the dancing tongues of fire. Then, into the circle stepped a tall man dressed entirely in red. From the tip of his high-crowned Stetson to his shiny boots, every aspect of this spectre from hell was blood-red.

Flat Nose Jack Bowdrie! And wearing a judge's horsehair wig.

'Is this the one?'

The soulless monotone echoed round the gathered throng.

Again.

'Is this the one who shot you down?'

'That's him.' The flat reply came from behind.

George Coward swung on his heel. His bulging eyes stared. His mouth hung open as he recognized the second speaker.

Cyrus Grant!

'What is your verdict members of the jury?'

'Guilty!' The decision of the macabre gathering, lifeless and devoid of emotion, echoed round the clearing.

'And is that the verdict of you all?'

'It is.'

'And what sentence should be passed on the accused?'

'*Death . . . Death . . . Death. . . .*'

It was not the dour throbbing chant that woke Bronco Travis from his recurrent nightmare. Having suffered the baleful imagery for the last four years, he knew only too well the horrific ending.

Sweat poured down his face. His breath came in short gasps. Staring ahead, he expected to see the noose swinging from a roof beam.

Nothing.

So what had propelled him beyond the realms of demonic insensibility?

An alien noise picked at his confused brain. There it was again. Outside the window, on the veranda.

Then it hit him. Somebody was trying to raise the sash.

It had to be one of Bowdrie's gang.

Quick as a flash, Bronco leapt out of bed and quietly positioned himself to the left of the window. Was it luck or fate that had made him close it on such a sultry night? He dispatched a silent prayer of thanksgiving to whatever god was up there, Maybe the guy was on his side after all.

Slowly the lower section of the window began to rise. A squeal of ungreased wood brought it to an abrupt halt. A sharp intake of breath came from the veranda. Then the window continued its upward journey. Bronco prepared himself. Gently he lifted the Henry repeating rifle above his head.

Holding his breath, he waited.

A hand appeared, clutching a long Bowie knife. The steel blade glinted in the moonlight. Without further hesitation, Bronco slammed the wooden stock of the rifle down on to the exposed arm. The intruder shrieked in pain, releasing the knife. It fell to the floor with a hollow thud. Grabbing hold of a sleeve, Bronco attempted to drag the intruder inside the room.

A fierce tussle ensued.

But desperation begets desperate measures. The assailant smashed the window with the butt of his revolver and pumped two shells into the room. Luckily for Bronco, the darkness ensured his safety. Flinging himself sideways away from the line of fire and splintering glass, he was forced to release the man. The bullets whistled harmlessly by, burying themselves in the opposite wall.

By the time he had recovered, and gingerly stuck his head out of the broken window, the prowler had disappeared. Although he had not been able to identify the man, he had no doubt that the attempted break-in had been instigated by Jack Bowdrie. Breathing heavily, he hauled himself over to the dresser and splashed cold water over his face.

A loud rapping on the door was accompanied by a pressing enquiry.

'You all right, Mr Travis?' It was the proprietor of the Wyman. 'I heard shots and breaking glass.' The knocking became more insistent, the enquiry more urgent. 'Please open up immediately. Otherwise I will have no alternative but to have my porter force the lock.'

'OK, OK. I'm a-comin'.' The response was a weary drawl.

Unlocking the door, Bronco let her in.

'You look like you've seen a ghost,' averred Lily May on

witnessing Bronco's wet and unkempt appearance. The
hunted look behind his sunken eyes gave his face a death-
like quality.

'You ain't far wrong there, ma'am,' agreed Bronco
smoothing down his lank hair. 'Some guy tried to rob me,
but luckily I scared him off.'

'I'll get the marshal,' answered Lily May casting an
apprehensive look towards the heap of broken glass. 'You
could have been killed.'

'No point,' replied Bronco rather too quickly. 'Probably
some drunk who saw me handing out free drinks at the
Bent Elbow and figured I was worth rolling. And I could-
n't identify him anyway.'

If Jack Bowdrie had managed to put the fear of God
into half the town, then he'd more'n likely have the
lawdog in his pocket. And the last thing Bronco needed
was to have the law nosing into his affairs. Not yet anyway.

'I'll clear up the mess in the morning and pay for a new
window,' he continued, ushering the woman gently from
the room. 'Nobody will bother me again tonight. Now that
he's been rumbled.'

'You sure you're all right?'

'If it makes you feel any better,' he offered with an
ironic twist, 'I'll sleep with one eye open and a shooter in
each hand.' He winked impishly. 'Done that more'n
once.'

When the lady of the house and her nighthawk had
departed, Bronco checked the veranda to assure himself
that it was indeed clear. Then he carefully scooped up
some loose glass and placed it on the window ledge. Any
further nocturnal visits and he would have ample warning.

Slumping on to the rumpled bed, he instantly fell
asleep. Thankfully, there was to be no recurrence of the

haunting visions that had so often dogged his nights of late.

'What in the name of Satan does it need to get rid of one man.'

Jack Bowdrie was angry. The veins on his neck pulsed, the twitching face was purple with rage. He slammed a bunched fist down on the large mahogany desk, upsetting a tumbler of whiskey. It went unheeded, Stalking round the side of the desk, he prodded his underlings with an evil glare.

'Some festerin' sore of a drifter swans into town figurin' he can do just as he pleases. And you bunch of greenhorns let him get away with it,' stormed Bowdrie, in full flow. But his diatribe brought no response. Nobody was about to draw the gunhawk's attention when he was in this mood.

It was obvious even to a casual observer that Flat Nose Jack Bowdrie had prospered during his years in Silverton. He had come a long way since quitting the fight game. His hand drifted unknowingly to his nose, distorted as a result of too many contests as a bare-knuckle boxer.

Rich drapes covered the office windows. Expertly crafted furniture complemented the sartorial elegance which the gang boss aspired. Specks of blue light reflected off the natty silk vest, accentuating the hard, cobalt eyes. It was an image in which Bowdrie revelled – hypnotic yet deadly, the ultimate predator.

And now he could avail himself of those Havana cigars he had always coveted. He pulled hard on the brown tube, funnelling a plume of blue smoke into the sweat-beaded face of Gomez.

'You,' he pointed an accusing finger at the Mexican,

'can't even handle a young kid without him removing half your ear.'

Gomez shuffled his feet uncomfortably, his eyes fixed on the thick carpet. A large white bandage covered the left side of his face.

Bowdrie emitted a snort of derision, then shifted his attention to the man on his left.

'And now this heap of dung comes a-crawling back here with a broken wrist.'

'Weren't my fault, boss,' whined Luke Trumper, a small weasel with a pointed snout and close-set shifty eyes. He clutched the injured joint, his face screwed up in pain. 'The guy must have second sight.'

Bowdrie grabbed him by the neckerchief, almost hoisting the little runt off the floor.

'I don't want excuses,' he ranted, his snarling visage so close he could smell Trumper's rancid breath. He recoiled visibly. 'I want action. And I want this jasper to know who's running this town.' Bowdrie's voice had risen an octave as the anger poured out. 'Now get out of my sight while I figure this out.'

He threw the little guy aside, forgotten. Trumper quickly left the room to lick his wounds. And seek the aid of the croaker. Afterwards, a few slugs of Red Label at the Bent Elbow would help ease the pain.

Following the murder of Henry Coward, Bowdrie had made it clear to the town dignitaries that he was in charge. And that if they played ball with him, life could proceed as before. With a few minor changes.

The first of these was to appoint Tom Gadds as the new town marshal, full-time and at a salary commensurate with such a responsible office, paid from town funds, of course.

He had soon discovered that Dan Tanner was not averse

to lining his own pockets at the town's expense, a situation Bowdrie fully exploited by making him mayor of Baker's Park. This new official likewise deserved a suitable remuneration. Kept strictly between the two of them were details of certain undisclosed sums paid into Tanner's bank account. Being the only assay agent, it was his job to value any silver ore that passed through his office. The exorbitant commission was split with Bowdrie.

Yes indeed, Flat Nose was well pleased with life in Silverton. And he had no intention of allowing some jumped-up squirt to upset the apple cart.

The Bowdrie Gang's arrival in Baker's Park back in 1869 had not been only for the purpose of exacting revenge. Flat-Nose had discovered the existence of a new silver lode in the Animas Valley. An over-talkative prospector had learned too late that sharing a secret was not a wise decision. His bones were now lying at the bottom of Bearclaw Ravine.

Ensuring that his was the only freight haulage business in town, Bowdrie had encouraged new prospectors to stake their claims. He was then able to control the shipment of ore down to the smelter at Durango. And his freight charges were such as to provide a more than comfortable life in the burgeoning town of Silverton.

Brick Stringer was the only other person in the office who displayed no fear. He had been with Bowdrie from the beginning. Together, the pair had broken out of the Denver pen. The big guy had saved Bowdrie's hide on more than one occasion and was now a sort of bodyguard, protecting the boss's rear. And he was the only member of the inner circle on whom Bowrie knew he could depend.

He handed Stringer a cigar – a gesture that affirmed the regard. Lighting up, Stringer savoured the superior

taste, nodding his appreciation. Life had likewise signifi-
cantly improved for the ex-railroad labourer since the duo
had paired up.

Bowdrie drew the big man aside.

'Tomorrow, I want you and Dutch Bob to pay this
pilgrim a visit.' He paused dramatically. An expressive
narrowing of the eyes plainly conveyed his meaning.

'I'm with you, boss,' sniggered Stringer, dragging on
the cigar. 'You can count on me.'

'And keep things quiet. No need to let the whole town
in on the action. Pretty Boy might well be the law around
here. But we still need to maintain a respectable appearance.' Bowdrie's tone lightened as he added; 'Can't have
the town council soiling its underwear, can we?'

A deep rumble of laughter shook the room.

'Wouldn't that be a sight,' warbled Stringer. Then he
left the room to locate the cold and calculating Dutch Bob
van Haagen. An immigrant from Europe, the man from
Amsterdam had ruthlessly proved his worth to the
Bowdrie Gang with his stock-in-trade, the deadly garrotte.

The ideal silencer!

Bowdrie scowled, his mouth an ugly slash. Perhaps now
he could resume the business of amassing the funds he
needed to quit this ugly berg for good. The bright lights of
San Francisco had beckoned invitingly for too long.

After breakfast the next morning, Bronco decided that
extreme measures were needed regarding his appearance.
Busting horses for the army had taken up all his time and
energy. At the end of each day, there had been little incli-
nation to bother with the finer points of personal hygiene.

And, much as he hated to admit the fact, those two
cowhands had been right. He did smell like a dung heap.
Halfway down Blair, he noticed a red-painted barber's

pole. That was what was needed. A haircut and full soak with some fancy-smelling lotion.

Swaggering along the boardwalk, boots clacking on the uneven slats, Bronco noticed a familiar figure emerge from the building on the opposite side of the street – the Blue Lagoon. It must be the one where Jack Bowdrie had made his headquarters. The guy stopped, a smug expression beneath the untidy growth of stubble.

Gomez again! And with him, a jigger with his right arm encased in a sling. Bronco smiled broadly. He couldn't resist the chance to heckle the pair of slimy toads.

'You fellers need to take more care,' he crowed. 'Hear what I say, Gomez?' His next comment was aimed at the second man. 'No 'arm done eh, *hombre*?' Bronco chuckled gleefully at his own wit.

Luke Trumper growled, his free hand dropping to the sixgun tucked into his belt. Gomez quickly restrained the rash impulse.

'Easy there, *amigo*,' he warned, the rhythmic tone quiet yet compelling. 'Not on thee main street. There will be another time, another place. Never fear. And eet will be of our choosing.'

Trumper grimaced, standing his ground. Slivers of hate flew across the busy street. Then he allowed himself to be hustled away in the opposite direction.

Bronco gave them a snort of derision, then headed for the barber's shop. He was the first customer of the day. A short rotund fellow in black serge trousers and a crisp white shirt bade him welcome. In fact it was the hair that grabbed Bronco's attention. A mite too smooth, and black as pitch. And that join . . .'

The dude was wearing a wig!

Stifling a chortle, he allowed himself to be led into the

emporium. Piggy eyes blinked at the newcomer from behind round wire-rimmed spectacles. In fact, everything about this little guy was circular.

'Let me take your coat and hat, sir,' twittered the little man, fussing about like a mother hen. 'Willie Mac at your service. Haircut, shave and a relaxing bath. All for the bargain price of one dollar.' He ushered Bronco to a seat, deftly flicking a protective gown over his body. 'Not that you need a bath, of course. Some clients only want a hair-cut, or maybe a shave.'

'Stop yer warblin' and get on with it,' rapped Bronco acidly. 'I'll have the whole caboodle.' Then he nodded towards one of several pictures pinned to the wall. 'And give me one of them there centre partings, with lots of oil to slick it down.'

He smiled at himself in the mirror, preening like a turkey cock. He deserved a bit of luxury after six months busting wild broncs. And with a new set of duds, perhaps he would pay that Murphy gal down at the livery a social call. She sure was a looker. Maybe he could persuade her to go for a buggy ride, take a picnic.

Then he remembered the reason for his reappearance in Silverton. This was no time to become complacent. Already, after only two days, there had been as many attempts to discourage his sojourn. Youthful exuber-ance was racing ahead of caution and a clear vision of what needed to be done. There was nothing so valuable to a man as experience. And Bronco Travis was sadly lacking in that department. He considered himself handy with a gun. But guile and cunning were essential when dealing with sly critters of Flat Nose Jack Bowdrie's ilk.

A lancing shiver rippled down the young man's spine.

He began to wonder what sort of bear pit he had wandered into.

'Yes, sir,' chirped the barber, breaking into his meditations and wielding a soap-laden shaving brush. 'You have excellent taste. The *Debonair* is the style I was about to suggest myself. A perfect choice for the man-about-town. And you will most assuredly be that when you leave here.' More foam was accompanied by a tuneful whistle. 'Not that you aren't already, you understand,' hurried on Willie Mac. 'A handsome gent, I mean. . . .'

Bronco sucked in a deep draught of oxygen. The dude was at it again.

'You from back East then?'

The blunt interjection immediately stemmed the flow. He was trying to place the barber's accent.

'No. I am English born and bred,' puffed the barber, equally thankful for the distraction. 'I always wanted to visit the Wild West after reading about it back home in Liverpool. So when the opportunity to emigrate arose, I grabbed it with both hands. And here I am,' the little man cooed, brandishing the soap-laden brush with a flourish as if he were an artist daubing a canvas.

Bronco was impressed. He had never encountered anybody from the old country before. The Travis clan had come over from England to escape religious persecution. But that was before he was born. His mother had often amused him with stories that her parents had passed down.

'My full name is actually William Macauley Trenton,' chirped the barber, slapping on more foam. 'A mouthful, I'm sure you agree. And not really what you would call very American. So I shortened it to Willie Mac. Much more acceptable under the circumstances.'

Just then, the light dimmed as another customer filled the doorway. Broad as he was tall with a heavy black beard and straggly hair, he was followed by a thin beanpole. The second man had a gaunt look. Yellow skin like parchment was drawn tightly across the angular skull.

Facing the wall, Bronco sensed rather than saw the pair.

'Good m-m-morning, g-gentlemen,' stammered the barber bobbing about like a cork on a rough pond. 'Please take a seat and I will be with you as s-s-soon as I am finished here.'

As the barber returned to his task, Bronco couldn't help noticing a thin film of sweat coating the barber's round face. Willie Mac set the mug down, then reached for a cut-throat razor and began to sharpen it on a leather strop. The whistling had become more of a choking rasp. And his beady eyes kept flitting about, never settling for an instant. The guy was jumpy as a cricket on heat.

And it was only since the other customers had entered. Bronco frowned, a puzzled expression lurking around the narrowed eyes.

'You feelin' well?' enquired Bronco.

'Just a touch on the w-warm side,' croaked Willie Mac, dabbing at his brow with a towel.

The razor hand descended. It was shaking. Bronco cast a wary peeper at the quaking barber, particularly that lethal bit of steel. The man was scared witless.

Then he saw it. A movement was reflected in the thick glass of the spectacles. It could only be . . .

Quick as a lunging sidewinder, he spun the chair on its greased axle whilst palming the Frontier.

'You gentlemen looking for me?'

He didn't wait for their reply. A knotted piece of cord in the hands of the skull man, and the hulk's brandishing a double-edged blade said it all.

Another of Bowdrie's efforts at persuasion.

The .44 Colt spoke its own language. The crash of gunfire reverberated round the small room. Two shots simultaneously found their mark. The two would-be assassins grunted with the deadly impact of hot lead. Any effort to stem the blood welling from shattered chest cavities was futile as their life force rapidly faded. Staggering backwards, both attackers plunged through the glass frontage of the barber's shop. Landing in an untidy heap on the dusty street, the bodies twitched momentarily, then were still.

As he tripped over a stool, Willie Mac uttered a fearful. screech. His black peruke parted company from the exposed bald pate. The sight of it glistening under the warming rays of the morning sun was too much for Bronco.

The pathetic and the ridiculous side by side. It was like a music-hall farce. Bronco burst into a fit of uncontrollable laughter. Death affects men differently. Caught in this bizarre circumstance, it was the only way his mind could handle the release of tension.

It was just unfortunate that Marshal Gadds chose that moment to appear in the shop doorway.

SEVEN

PAYING THE PRICE

'Drop that there hogleg, pilgrim,' hissed Gadds, adopting his most menacing stance. 'And make it slow and easy. There's two dead men out here and I don't figure that for a joke.'

The smile on Bronco's face paled as the realization of his situation sunk in. He was still sitting in the barber's chair, the white smock boasting a pair of singed bullet holes round his neck. But triumph was rapidly turning into tragedy, farce into sobriety.

'I said drop that smokepole, mister.' Gadds wagged his own shooter, edging carefully into the barber's emporium. 'Else that sheet's gonna be acquiring a chamberful of fresh holes.'

The revolver hit the floor with a dull thud.

Gadds gave a satisfied nod then turned to address the trembling barber.

'What happened here, Willie?'

Naturally fastidious when it came to personal appearance, William Macaulay Trenton had completely forgotten that his treasured peruke – tailor-measured and hand-made in St Louis – was now residing in a pool of blood on the floor. Nobody had ever been privy to his lack of hair before. This was his first taste of the Wild West at close quarters. And it left a bad taste in the mouth. The little guy was in shock.

'Well?' snapped Gadds. 'Spit the grief, will yuh.'

'Y-yes, of course, Marshal,' stuttered Willie, scrambling to his feet. His normally florid cheeks were grey like rotten meat. He felt sick. 'Those men were going to . . . to . . . molest this gentleman.'

'Molest? What d'yuh mean, molest!' thundered Bronco flinging the smock aside. 'Them sneakin' polecats was after a termination. And a quiet one at that.'

'How do you figure that?' asked Gadds, keeping his gun firmly pointed in Bronco's direction.

'Look there.' Bronco jabbed a finger at the two items resting beside the ruined headpiece. There was no smile this time. 'A garotte if I'm not mistaken, and that Bowie wasn't for trimmin' no fingernails.'

'Uhmm!' muttered Gadds, trying to inject some degree of scepticism into the grunt. He was well aware that the two dead men had worked for Bowdrie. Brick Stringer and he went back a long way. Bob van der Haagen was a new recruit. The Dutchman had only recently joined the payroll and they had never actually had words. Now they never would. The marshal also knew that Bowdrie was having trouble with this particular fellow.

A crowd had gathered outside the barber's. More than one onlooker couldn't resist smirking at Willie Mac's discomfort.

'Could that be a turkey egg you're wearin', Willie?'

jeered one joker at the rear. Laughs all round. These jiggers were used to gunplay in Silverton.

'Looks more like a baby's rear end to me,' another humorist sniggered.

The colour had returned to the barber's face with a vengeance as embarrassment at discovering his personal loss struck home.

Gadds was not amused.

'Anybody here see what happened?' he enquired brusquely, hoping for a universal shaking of heads.

'It's just as Willie Mac said,' called a raised voice close by. It was Sunset Johnson. 'Them fellas was tryin' to sneak up on this man from behind. I saw it all through the window. But he was too darned quick for 'em.' Sunset whistled his appreciation. 'Ain't seen gunplay like that since Clay Alison was bested down in Cimarron. Now that was some duel.'

Johnson chirruped at the dreamy reminiscence. He had a ready-made audience. Everybody enjoyed a good tale so no further encouragement was necessary.

'Clay was so taken aback when Mace Bowman beat him to the draw that he challenge the guy to a gun-dance in bare feet. Never seen nothin' like it. Stripped down to their underwear they was. First to move lost the contest and had to stand the whole saloon a drink.'

'Cut the gaff, you old soak,' slammed Gadds impatiently. 'I got no time for your fairy tales.' Then he turned his attention back to Bronco. A scowl marred the spruce image. There was going to be more trouble to come with this dude. He could sense it. But on the evidence, he couldn't hold him.

'Well,' declared the marshal somewhat reluctantly, 'it appears you are in the clear. That is if these fellers tried to kill you.'

'Of course they did,' huffed Bronco.

'You're free to go. But watch your step in future. We don't cotton to gun-happy sharpshooters in Silverton.'

Bronco bit his lip, resisting the temptation to remind this turkey that it was he who had almost been killed here. He set his hat on hair that was still lank and greasy, sniffed at his grey flannel shirt that still reeked of horse, and realized that he must resemble Santa Claus with a stubbled face caked in shaving-foam. Grabbing at the cloth round his neck he removed the white beard.

The situation that had minutes previously seemed nonsensical was now striking home with the force of a rampant bull. Two men had died. Skulking bushwhackers maybe, but that didn't make it any easier to handle.

'I'll be needing a name to enter on the report,' said Gadds, licking the end of a pencil.

Bronco met his gaze evenly.

'I go under the handle of Bronco Travis,' he averred shrugging into his coat and retrieving his floored pistol. 'But there's some round here who might recall my real name.' He reined in the dialogue, ready to gauge the marshal's reaction. Then he shot from the hip. 'It's George Coward.'

Gadds' expression remained flat, inscrutable. Then he tensed. His tawny eyes flinched, staring. Only for an instant, but long enough for Bronco to witness a haunting fear impress itself on the marshal's psyche, a recollection of the nightmare he thought had been left far behind.

Pretty Boy Gadds had played his own gruesome role in Henry Coward's brutal demise. And he had regretted his involvement ever since. Although it hadn't stopped him accepting the prestigious marshal's job. The years in between had taught Gadds the meaning of respect, admiration even. Especially from the few females who inhabited the town. He was loath to surrender such esteem. Now here was the critter who could force just that.

Gadds quickly turned away to conceal his anxiety. The fun was over and the crowd was dispersing. He directed a quartet of the more inquisitive to remove the corpses to the funeral parlour. Then he slunk off to inform his boss of the grim news none of them wanted to hear.

By this time, Willie Mac had recovered his composure, and his beloved hair.

'Who is going to pay for all this damage?' he lamented, short arms gesticulating crazily.

Bronco surveyed the interior with a jaundiced eye.

'Send the bill to Jack Bowdrie,' he suggested lazily. 'His boys were the cause of it.'

The barber sighed grumpily then set about clearing up. Sunset Johnson took Bronco by the elbow.

'You must be Henry Coward's son,' he exclaimed with an impassioned ardour. It was a statement rather than a question. 'Your pa was well regarded all through the valley. It was pure bloody murder what they done to him.' Sunset hung his head in shame. His next utterance, bleak and woeful, was a confession from the soul.

'I was one of them in the crowd. None of us brave townsfolk lifted a finger. We just stood there and allowed a heroic man to be killed. You may be named Coward, but it's us what bear the stigma. It did for me, son, I can tell you. Turned me from a successful chicken farmer into the liquored-up bum that stands before you now.'

Bronco couldn't help but sympathize with the old-timer. He patted him on the back trying to alleviate some of the agony oozing from his every pore. But no amount of remorse could alter the past. What was done was done. And there were too many in this goddamned berg who had every wish to see him buried in the same graveyard as his father.

The chiselled features set hard in a stony mask. Bronco was well aware that the advantage of surprise had now been lost. He would need to have eyes in the back of his head from here on. He cast a sorry eye at the wretched individual beside him.

'Here, Sunset.' He took out a silver dollar and placed in the grubby palm. 'Looks to me like you could do with a good meal inside you.'

'Much obliged,' responded the swamper, more relieved by the placatory gesture than by the money itself. He lowered his voice to a scratchy whisper, adding: 'Bowdrie and his gang are gonna come looking for you now, George. Last thing they want is old crimes being resurrected. You need a place to hide out. Give you some breathing space to decide how best to proceed.'

'That's good advice, old-timer,' replied Bronco. 'You got anywhere in mind?'

'Sure have.' Johnson perked up, anxious to help out. 'You can use my old place. It's no mansion house. But it's habitable. Best of all though, none of Bowdrie's sidewinders knows about it.'

He then went on to describe the cabin's location in a side valley up around the Red Mountain area called Gila Bend.

Recognizing the truth of Sunset Johnson's deliberations, Bronco moseyed on down to the Wyman. Pushing through the noisy bustle of miners on the sidewalk, his hawkish eyes flitted every which way, searching for the confrontation he knew would come. Then again, maybe it would be a bullet in the back. They had already tried to ambush him in the barber's.

Sweat broke out on his face. He quickened his pace.

He paid his bill at the hotel, much to the disappointment of the gushing hostess, and left. His next visit was to the livery stable. He prayed hard that nothing had happened to Blaze during his absence.

Ben Murphy was sweeping up loose hay.

'How has Blaze been?' enquired a concerned Bronco Travis.

'Just dandy. You sure know how to pick a fine animal, Mr Travis.' The ostler paused. He could sense that something was amiss. 'You were right about Bowdrie. He was more bothered about you crossing him than with the chestnut. All the same, I did move her into an adjoining stall. Hope you don't mind?'

Their earlier problem was small change now.

'You ain't heard, then?'

Murphy's face creased in a puzzled frown.

'Heard what?'

'Gunfire up at Willie Mac's barber shop.'

'Guns are going off all the time in Silverton these days. I don't pay it no mind.' All the same, Ben Murphy struggled to hold his curiosity in check.

Bronco stroked the muzzle of the chestnut, whispering softly into her nostrils, just like he'd been taught all those years ago by Clint Weaver at the Rocking-Chair. Then he turned back to the ostler.

'Can you saddle her up while I go buy some provisions?'

Murphy nodded. 'Sure thing. Where you going?'

'Sunset Johnson's place at Gila Bend.'

Bronco departed, leaving the ostler to continue his work. He returned some two hours later.

Ellen Murphy was brushing Blaze. The horse sighed with contentment, far removed from the cares of the world in which her master was embroiled.

'She likes you,' he murmured.

The girl turned. A fetching smile lit up her oval face.

'Kindness and reassurance. That's all. It's the same with animals as well as humans. We all need to be cared for.' She peered deep into the young man's eyes. Black holes, tormented and full of hurt, stared back.

'What is it, Bronco?' Ellen took hold of his hand. The sensation was electric. His whole body tingled.

Then he told her.

After he had poured out his soul, Ellen felt inexplicably drawn to this enigmatic man. Instinctively she hugged him. Bronco was caught unawares. He had known few women in his short life, mostly those who frequented the pleasure houses attached to saloons. A quick fumble and away.

This was different. It felt good. All the hate bottled up over the years dissolved, ebbing away. Encased in this woman's arms, even Jack Bowdrie was of secondary importance. Nobody had ever made him feel this way before.

But could he ever forget what that rannigan and his gang had done? Perhaps, given time. Although definitely not if he stayed in Silverton. One or other of them would end up in boot hill. That was no answer to anything. It was a dilemma with no apparent solution.

Ellen appeared to read his thoughts.

'Don't fret, Bronco,' she purred. 'The past is behind you. It's the future that matters now.'

Then she invited him for dinner that evening.

'We live just behind Empire Street at the north end of town. It's the only house with a white picket fence out front. Dad needs help running the business. For some time he's been meaning to take on an extra hand.' She offered a dazzling smile, her clear green eyes twinkling impishly. 'Perhaps I can persuade him that you are that person. That is if you intend sticking around.'

She gave him a searching look, her liquid eyes questioning. To Ellen Murphy, it all appeared so clear-cut. Forgive and forget. Bronco knew in his heart that life was never going to be that simple. He was of the mind that Bowdrie would never allow the situation to stumble on unresolved. Sooner or later, there would have to be a final reckoning, a confrontation. A dark shadow hung over his future.

But for the moment, at least, he could soak himself in Ellen Murphy's delightful company. Bathe in the warm glow of her magnetic allure.

Slowly, his proud bearing relaxed.

'I sure would like to set down some roots,' he said absorbing the exotic fragrance emanating from this desert orchid.

Ellen smiled gracefully. She offered him a peck on the cheek, then left him to bask in his dreams. Bronco sat himself down on a bale of straw and followed the girl's sedate progress until she disappeared amidst the noisy confusion of Blair Street. A dog yapped close by in pursuit of a ginger cat. Overhead grey clouds gathered. The low rumble of thunder in the distance heralded the approach of a storm. Was it a portent of things to come?

Bronco shook his head, trying to make sense of his feelings and his responsibilities. Could they be one and the same?

The wistful preoccupation was suddenly interrupted by a ragged-assed urchin tugging at his sleeve.

'You Mr Coward?' bleated the youngster.

Bronco was instantly alert. Few people were aware of his real identity.

'What of it'?' he rapped, standing up.

'I have a message for you.'

Bronco waited. The kid held out a grubby paw.

Breathing out a sigh, Bronco dug into his pocket and flicked a dime into the air. The kid caught it with an expertise born of frequent such panhandling.

'Jack Bowdrie, the guy with the mashed nose?' the kid squawked, clapping his hands in delight. 'He wants to meet with you. Settle things peacefully is what he said. You're to come to the Blue Lagoon at six this evening.'

Swinging on his heel, Bronco retired to the cool interior of the stable. There was much that needed thinking on. His features crinkled, mystification written across the lined forehead. Did Bowdrie really want to smoke the peace pipe? It seemed barely credible. Perhaps he didn't want trouble, anybody rocking the boat and interfering in his money-making schemes. He'd tried the hard way three times and failed.

'What did that kid want?' Ben Murphy called out from the end stall.

'Seems like Bowdrie wants a powwow.'

Murphy scratched his grey head, the square jaw tightening.

'I'd trust that snake-in-the-grass as much as a cardsharp on pay day.' The terse remark was brusque and to the point. 'My advice is to keep well away.'

'Sunset Johnson has offered me the use of his cabin,' said Bronco, arriving at the same conclusion. 'Figure I'll head out that way tomorrow morning.'

'Good idea. Give you time to think things through.' Murphy eyed the younger man casually. 'Ellen appears to have taken a shine to you.'

'Uhmm!' Bronco's response was non-committal, although his face coloured slightly.

'She's a fine cook,' added Murphy, idly wielding a hay fork, 'and will pack you some victuals afore you leave for Gila Bend.'

Bronco coughed to hide his discomfort. He was no Lothario when it came to any dealings with the fairer sex.

'She says you need some help. How about I lend a hand here 'til supper time?'

Murphy stifled a smile before nodding towards another fork.

'Always use a strong pair of shoulders, that's for danged sure.'

At a quarter before six, Bronco excused himself, claiming he needed to wash up. He had considered his actions long and hard during the afternoon. And had decided to call Bowdrie's bluff, if such it was. One way or the other, he needed to learn the jasper's intentions.

Heading towards the Blue Lagoon, he checked the loading of his revolver and ensured it was loose in the holster. His whole body was tense, expectant, nerves stretched tight like a drawn bow. Black clouds scudded by overhead driven onward by a howling wind. Brilliant flashes of lightning splintered the air. Rain threatened but held itself in check.

Passing a narrow passage between two mercantiles, Bronco's attention was caught by a gesticulating figure. It was the young messenger again. Spasms of terror jerked the bobbing kid like some demented puppet on a string. He yelled an incoherent spew of gibberish, then scuttled off back down the alley.

The bizarre performance was for Bronco's benefit. Always the Good Samaritan where underdogs were concerned, his natural instinct was to dash to the rescue. The .44 Frontier palmed, he launched down the alley on the run. Rounding the corner at the back of the wooden building, he abruptly found himself splayed out on the floor. A heavy boot had unceremoniously tripped him up.

Out of the corner of his eye he could see the simpering urchin disappearing into the gloom. Then it struck him.

A set-up.

And he'd fallen for it – hook, line and sinker. There was no time to reflect on his gullibility. Heavy steel-capped boots slammed into his ribs. Their purpose, to inflict maximum damage. This was no casual ambush. He rolled over trying to avoid the pounding. But there was no escape. Legs all around thrashed and hammered at his exposed body. There must have been at least four assailants. Nobody spoke. Only the grim sound of wheezing grunts as each strove to land the hardest kick. These turkeys knew their business.

Then one of the attackers broke the silence.

'That's enough!' came the brusque command. Even through the haze of pain that a racked his battered torso, it was enough for Bronco. He recognized that voice.

Marshal Tom Pretty Boy Gadds.

But that was not the end of the beating. Only the beginning.

Hefty wooden staves began raining down. Bronco tried to scream. The agony was too great even for that. He knew the end was near. And there was nothing he could do about it. They say that with the approach of death a man's life flashes before his eyes. All Bronco was able to visualize were the whips scourging his father and the final blast of sixguns despatching him to the great beyond.

Was this likewise to be his fate? No chance to avenge the vile outrage?

A dark mist filtered down, smothering his blistered spirit. Consciousness was slipping away. He felt himself sliding into a black pit of despair. Yet still he held on. Perhaps he was already dead. Stuck in limbo, awaiting the descent into hell's inferno.

'Hold down his right hand.'

Gadd's voice again, a distant murmur from another dimension.

Seconds later a searing jolt of fire lanced through his hand, storming up his arm to blow his head off. Or so it seemed. A scorching blast of sheer agony erupted from his tortured soul.

'Gag him before anyone hears.' But the growled order came too late.

Somebody had already cocked an ear to the brutal fracas. Two shots cracked the ether. Splinters of wood sprayed from the building just above the heads of the aggressors.

A crack of lightning illuminated the grim tableau.

Three jiggers with raised clubs, another holding a hammer, crouched over a jumble of bleeding rags on the ground. They turned open-mouthed to face the untimely interruption. Two men were crouched on each side of the Blair Street entrance to the alley. Another pair of shots encouraged the gathering to disperse. One of the ambushers wasn't quick enough. Uttering a choked gasp he fell dead, blood pouring from his shattered skull.

That was enough. Fleeing in disarray down the alley, they dispersed like rats into the gloom of early evening.

Charily, fearful of any retaliation, the rescuers crept

down the passage, one wary step at a time. Gun at the ready, one of them bent over the groaning figure.

'Recognize him?'

'Cain' t tell. You got a light?'

A scraping of match on leather followed. In the resultant yellow glow, both men sucked in deep draughts of oxygen.

'Well, I'll be,' exclaimed Nevada Jones on recognizing the bronc rider. He could see at a glance that the young man was in a bad way. Turning to address his partner, he said; 'This feller needs help. You git on down to the livery and ask Murphy to send a buckboard.'

'Is he gonna live?' enquired Jim Finney, eyeballing the injured man.

'Don't ask such damn fool questions,' growled Jones, wiping some of the blood from Bronco's mashed face. 'Now git goin'!'

EIGHT

REST AND RECOVERY

In less than ten minutes. a freight wagon with a spare saddle-horse tied behind drew up alongside the groaning body. Ben Murphy jumped down, followed by the muttering figure of Old Virginny. The ostler had been in the process of closing up the livery barn for the night when the old miner had rushed in, arms a flapping like a rampant turkey. Valuable minutes were wasted trying to extract the gist of the story.

On learning that Bronco Travis had been brutally assaulted Murphy immediately assumed that this was Bowdrie's work. He hurried off to the alley the old-timer had described, approaching from the rear to avoid any prying eyes on the main street.

'What we gonna do?' voiced a panic-stricken Nevada Jones. 'This poor sap needs proper treatment else he'll die for sure.'

Murphy ignored the obvious. Instead, he indicated for the two miners to help him to lift the battered victim carefully into the well of the wagon. Speed was of the essence.

Any minute, those skunks might return to finish the job. He wrapped Bronco in a blanket to keep him warm. A large tarpaulin was then draped over the body of the wagon to hide its mangled contents.

'Will you two fellers accompany me with this cargo'?' Murphy enquired, climbing up on to the driving bench.

Both miners nodded eagerly. Finney clutched the Hawken rifle tightly to his chest anxiously peering about for any signs of a counter attack.

'Where you a-takin' him?' asked Jones.

'Sunset Johnson's place out at Gila Bend.' Murphy's reply was stiff, taut. He was keen to get away. 'Now hoist yourselves into the wagon beside Bronco. And keep out of sight. I want this to appear like any normal freight-hauling job.'

Quietly jigging the horses into motion, he set the wagon along the back of the stores to emerge on to Blair Street further up towards the start of Empire. His purpose was to avoid any suspicion.

Pretty Boy Gadds was looking decidedly nervous. He took another long pull from a bottle of rye whiskey. His smooth cheeks flushed a deep puce, tawny eyes bulging as the hard liquor tore a strip from his throat. He was sprawled rather than seated behind a battered old desk in his office, Stetson askew on his unruly thatch of brown hair. Following the untimely interruption of their assault on Bronco Travis, the bushwhackers had fled down the narrow passage behind the mercantiles, entering the jail-house through the back entrance.

Facing the marshal, expressions drawn and pale, were his two remaining conspirators.

'You shoulda killed him while you had the chance.'

95

This outburst came from Butte Madison, a young hothead who had joined the Bowdrie gang hoping to expand his billfold without the need for hard graft. Following an abortive single-handed attempt to rob a stagecoach in his home state of Montana, Madison had taken to accosting lone riders on the trail. Rarely did these robberies net more than a few dollars. He was hoping there would be easier pickings in Silverton.

'*Sí, hombre,*' agreed Gomez, prodding a thick finger at the marshal. 'Why you a-smash hees gunhand when a bullet in thee head was better?'

The other man, Cross-eyed Buck Flannery leaned against the wall and said nothing. Not known for his output of oratory, Flannery's cold demeanour spoke for him.

Gadds took another slug of whiskey. In reality, he did not want any more killing on his patch. His intention had been for a severe beating to encourage the interloper in the belief that Silverton was not a place to linger. The intervention of the two rescuers had effectively stymied that plan.

'It ees best to tell thee boss soon what happened,' advised Gomez, shaking his head. 'And I am theenking he weel not be moocho pleased.'

'Why me?' whined Gadds, tipping the bottle. 'We was all there.'

'It's you that's wearin' the tin star, *Marshal,*' snapped Madison, hiding a leery smirk.

Gadds sniffed. He sunk one last slug and hoisted himself somewhat unsteadily to his feet. Setting his hat straight, he lurched towards the door.

'Good luck, Marshal.' This parting shot from Madison was followed by a gruff chortle.

*

Murphy drew the wagon to a halt at the entrance to Blair Street. He peered hesitantly up and down the crowded thoroughfare, trying to spot any unwelcome curiosity. Nothing seemed out of the ordinary. Tinny piano music echoed from a half a dozen drinking-parlours. Raucous laughter mingled with curses as the lengthening shadows of approaching darkness settled over the town.

The ostler eventually found a gap in the chaotic milieu and pulled out, heading north. Hat pulled down to hide his face, Murphy's hawkish gaze flicked from side to side.

A choking groan suddenly broke from beneath the tarpaulin. Murphy stiffened.

'Keep him quiet under there,' he hissed. ''We can't afford to draw any attention to ourselves. Bowdrie's knuckleheads could be anywhere.'

That was when he saw Gadds. The marshal was heading straight towards them. His gait was rather erratic as he shouldered other pedestrians aside. He appeared to be staring directly at the suspect wagon. Murphy sucked in his breath, muscles screwed up in a tangled knot. Another pained croak from the injured Travis was choked off by the two guardians. It still sounded loud enough to wake the dead.

Nobody paid them any heed. And then Gadds disappeared into the subdued interior of the Blue Lagoon. Murphy breathed again as they drew away from the danger zone.

Inside the sultry interior of the Blue Lagoon, Gadds sidled up to the bar. Bowdrie and the mayor were huddled together at the far end. There appeared to be some altercation between them. In between, a nondescript clutch of loafers hunkered over their drinks. Even in the close smoky atmosphere of the saloon, Gadds felt an icy chill surge through his bones. A film of sweat glistened on his handsome face. This was one time he would have gladly swapped the marshal's job for that of a night-soil humper.

'I don't like this killing, Jack.' Dan Tanner drew himself off the bar, assuming an official stance. 'It's giving the town a bad name.'

'So how do you suggest I deal with this jumped-up rannie?'

'Pay him off like you have done every other trouble-maker what's hit town.'

'This dude is Coward's kin,' spat Bowdrie, his saturnine features writhing irritably. 'He's after giving me a one-way trip to visit the pearly gates. Or have you conveniently forgotten that little set-to back in '69.'

'Well, I don't like it,' repeated Tanner forcefully.

A lurid growl spewed from Bowdrie's throat. He suddenly grabbed the mayor by his finely tailored silk shirt. Buttons popped as the expensive material ripped along the seam.

'Now listen here, you bloated windbag,' snarled the gang boss, his angular nose inches from the other's. Tanner could almost taste the malodorous breath, but dared not flinch under the piercing gaze. 'Since throwing in with me, you've become rich and fat, living the high life. It's me what's fed you all the tasty morsels. And it's me that decides what's to be done around this stinking berg. You jump when I say. Got that?'

Another violent squeeze on the mayor's constricted windpipe elicited a hoarse croak. 'Just remember, you're in this up to your scrawny neck. And don't you ever forget it.' A casual shove deposited the gasping mayor on the seat of his tight pants. 'Now get out of my sight.'

Tanner was not slow in complying. He scrambled to his feet and quickly backed off to leave through a side door clutching at his aching throat.

Swallowing hard, Tom Gadds shrugged off his edginess and approached the gang boss. Drawing to a halt behind, he coughed.

Bowdrie looked round, thick eyebrows raised questioningly.

'I gotten something to tell yuh, boss.' The marshal's tremulous voice betrayed the fact that it was bad news.

Bowdrie's teeth clenched, thin lips warped into a snarl.

'Not here,' he spat, nodding for them to retire to a side booth, and out of earshot.

'Well?' snapped Bowdrie, drawing the blue velvet curtains shut.

In a faltering bleat, Gadds relayed the events of the ambush, omitting to mention his disquiet with regard to the proposed killing. His palms were sticky, shifty eyes searching for the explosion he knew was coming.

'What are we going to do about this Coward, or Travis as he's now called?' fretted Gadds, plucking at his tin star. 'Them snoopin' varmints will have spirited him away by now.'

Bowdrie waved him to silence, stroking his chin, deep in thought. He was now only too well aware that this damn-blasted asshole was going to be no pushover. He also realized that the critter had to be eradicated from the picture. His reputation depended on it. Already three of his men had been injured and the same number killed.

More of the same and rebellious elements in Silverton would begin to raise their ugly heads to challenge his position. Nevada Jones had already assumed the mantle of miners' leader and was inciting his dirt-scratchers to move their own loot. Others would quickly sense he was losing his grip.

'Make sure that guards are posted on all the trails out of town,' he announced after much deliberation. 'I want that bastard caught and out of my craw. Nobody enters or leaves without my say-so.' Bowdrie angled a look of mocking disdain at this excuse for a lawdog. 'Reckon you can manage that?'

'Sure thing, boss.' Gadds' relief at being let off the hook was palpable.

The gang leader dismissed him with a scornful flick of his bullet head.

Once beyond the town limits, Murphy relaxed. He drew back the tarpaulin. Although rutted and uneven, the trail north-west over Red Mountain Pass was wide and well-used. It was only when he had to turn off into the side valley of Gila Bend that he reined in the horses to an even trot. By this time, the black mantle of night had settled over the landscape. Dark banks of fir rose up on either side, hemming them into the narrow trail. A full moon afforded sufficient illumination for the ostler to maintain a steady pace.

Few people came this way as the valley tapered into a box canyon three miles beyond the clearing where Sunset Johnson had built his cabin. An hour after forking off the main road, the wagon drew to a halt beside Indian Rock.

One hazard remained.

The approach to the lonely farmhouse was barely wide enough for the freight wagon to pass. Here, for 200 yards, the valley closed in to allow of no more than a narrow track before opening out into a level grassy clearing. The wheel hubs scraped against the rock wall that rose sheer on either side. The discordant grating of steel on rock set their teeth on edge. Hands clamped over bursting eardrums, it was a welcome relief to emerge into the wholesome quiet of the clearing.

Rich grassland stretched away towards the edge of the clearing a mile up valley. After that, the tree curtain closed in once again.

Jones clapped his hands.

'Never knew this place existed.' His slack jaw quivered in wondrous admiration. 'Feller could set down roots here.'

'Sunset kept it a secret after his family left,' replied Murphy, pondering on the ex-chicken farmer's slide down life's slippery slope.

'What happened then?'

'Don't rightly know,' drawled the ostler, pulling the team to halt outside the cabin.

In truth, Charlie Johnson's wife had abandoned the family home following her husband's decline into the dubious delights of Red Label whiskey. Taking her two children, she had returned to Kansas City where her folks lived.

The once prosperous chicken business had since disintegrated. Only a handful of scrawny fowl now survived. And each time Sunset had returned to the cabin, there was one less following his return to Silverton and the grubby storeroom behind the Bent Elbow which he now called home.

The squawk of chickens informed them that they were drawing close to the cabin.

'Let's be gettin' this jigger inside,' asserted Jones, hoisting Bronco's recumbent form by the shoulders and indicating for Old Virginny to take his legs.

Inside the plank door, Murphy fired up a vesta and lit a coal-oil lantern hanging on a nail. The cabin was nothing short of a mess, uncared for, with a musty odour hanging in the air. An unctuous blend of sweat, grease and dampness vied for superiority. Unwashed crockery was piled high in the sink. A liberal coating of dust covered every surface. It was obvious that a woman's touch had been absent for some considerable time.

The miners hurried through to a back room. They smoothed out the heap of grubby blankets on the double bed and carefully settled Bronco down. After stripping off his bloody outer garments, Jones examined the mangled body.

He sucked in a lungful of air. It was not a pretty sight.

'This guy needs a sawbones,' he averred grimly. 'And soon.'

'I'll get a fire goin',' suggested Murphy, wrinkling his nose, 'then see if I can't sniff out some decent grub in this flea-pit. How anybody can live like this beats me.' His head shook in bewilderment.

The two old miners nodded simultaneously. Deadpan expressions concealed the fact that their own domestic arrangements were little better.

'While you're about it, heat up a pan of water,' said Nevada. 'We need to clean this feller up, find out how bad hurt he is.'

It was then that Murphy realized how much time had passed. Peering at his pocket watch, he gasped:

'Ellen will be worried sick. Bronco was to be our guest for dinner this evening. That was at seven o'clock.'

'Reckon it must be around midnight by now,' guessed Jones, casting a practised eye towards the twinkling canopy overhead.

'Midnight at least,' confirmed Virginny, nodding enthusiastically.

Murphy allowed himself a detached smile.

'Ten after to be precise,' he said. 'Are you fellers able to handle this on your own? I have to get back to town. Soon as possible, I'll send Doc Mathers to fix up his injuries.'

Jones threw him an anxious frown.

'Can he be trusted?'

'The doc and me go back a ways. Sound veter'nary as well. I'd trust him with my bank account, and my best horse.'

'OK by me then,' concurred Jones. 'But let's hope it don't come to that.'

After ensuring that the patient was as comfortable as could be expected, Murphy left. Bronco Travis had still not regained consciousness.

The oppressive mantle of night still shrouded the cabin when Jones was awoken by what he thought was the sole remaining rooster. He sat up, shaking the mud from between his ears. Too early for that. So it had to be something else.

A series of strident raps followed by a piercing shriek gave him the answer. Jerked fully awake, he lit a candle and scuttled through to the next room. Bronco was sitting up banging his head against the wall, face blanched white, eyes red and staring.

The nightmare had returned with increased ferocity.

Jones dabbed the blotchy face with a damp rag.

'Easy there, boy,' he cooed. 'The sawbones will be here soon.'

In fact it was another two hours before Doc Mathers arrived in his buckboard, accompanied by Ben Murphy. Being narrower than the freight wagon, it had easily negotiated the narrow ravine. Ellen trotted behind on her black stallion, barely able to control her impatience at their slow progress.

She had insisted on coming along after being acquainted with Bronco's severe beating. On first hearing the terrible news, she was all for riding out to Gila Bend without delay. No thought was given to the danger involved, either to herself or the man she now realized had captured her heart. Only the insistent urging of her father supported by the good doctor had persuaded the distraught girl that prudence and discretion needed to be observed.

Taking the direct route to Gila Bend was out of the question. Extreme caution had to be exercised when leaving Silverton so as not to arouse Bowdrie's suspicions.

Once the gang boss had discovered that his Nemesis had been spirited away, a search of every possible hideout had been undertaken. A lack of success had resulted in a guard being assigned to watch the main trails out of town.

Luckily for the doc and his associates there were a few less well-used trails, although they were much rougher, necessitating many detours. But Bronco's terminal methods of dealing with those sent to rub him out had left Bowdrie short-handed, and unable to cover them all. Marshal Gadds had decided for his own health not to inform the boss about these complications.

Nevertheless, it was not until the early hours that the trio had been able to slip away unnoticed. They reached the cabin as the false dawn was peeling away the black drape of night. Velvet indigo faded to purple as the new day surfaced above the lower peaks surrounding Red Mountain. The rooster announced their arrival – unmistakable on this occasion – just as a flight of lark-buntings scooted across the clearing in search of an early breakfast.

Inside the cabin, Doc Mathers quickly set to work examining the patient.

'Will he be all right?' Ellen's voice trembled. Liquid eyes, soft and pleading, expressed all that she now felt for this young man who had so abruptly entered her life.

'Let the doctor do his job,' said her father, his strong hands gently drawing the girl away and sitting her down on a chair.

'He's certainly been worked over,' sighed Mathers, expertly running sensitive fingers over the ravaged torso. It was another half-hour before he spoke again.

'Three broken ribs and a whole mountain of cuts and bruises,' he announced eventually, in a grave tone of voice. 'They will heal in a few weeks. But it's the right hand that is the problem. The tendons will set in time, but there'll be no more gunplay with that hand.' Then he added with a smile aimed at Nevada Jones and Virginny who were hunkered in the doorway. 'It's a good job you two showed up when you did, otherwise this guy would be on the mortuary slab at this moment.'

'But he will be all right?' pressed Ellen, clutching at the doc's shirt-sleeve.

'Strong young feller like that – don't see why he shouldn't make a full recovery.' The doc paused, slowly pulling on a black frock-coat. A dark shadow clouded the thoughtful features. 'He'll need a heap of nursing mind. No riding or excessive movement for at least a month.'

'I'll make certain he has the best care and attention anyone could give,' the girl avowed, softly stroking the long dark hair.

'Much obliged to you, Doc,' croaked Bronco wincing as a barb of pain shot through his smashed hand. His ashen features creased as he tried to sit up.

'Rest and recovery,' stated the medico firmly with a slow smile. 'And that's doctor's orders.'

Leaving some potions and a salve to be applied at regular intervals, he departed, promising to return to check on his patient in a week's time.

Ellen gently brushed the injured man's cheek with her lips. She gave a smile that left a thousand words unspoken. No amount of physical punishment could leave him insensible to her touch. After one last lingering gaze the pragmatic Ellen Murphy reasserted herself.

'Like the doctor said, you need to rest and let nature take its course.' She mopped the sweat from his fevered brow, then went into the front parlour. Food needed preparing and the cabin tidying.

It was abundantly clear that there was much to be done.

Bronco exhaled and sank back into the comfort of the warm bed. Paradoxically, sensations of helplessness and fulfilment pervaded his thoughts.

Even through the mist of pain that plagued his body, he knew that life could never be the same again. He had at last found someone who could dispel the haunting visions that constantly assailed his sleeping hours. And she appeared to have the same feelings for him. He also knew there could be no future for either of them while Jack Bowdrie was around to play havoc with his mind and body.

And there was only one solution to that problem.

NINE

THE PENNY DROPS

Jack Bowdrie was becoming increasingly frustrated. It was three weeks since George Coward, or Bronco Travis, had been attacked, and had effectively disappeared from the scene.

Since then – nothing. Not a word. No clue as to what had happened to him. Was he dead? Had he slunk away, cowed and defeated? Until Bowdrie knew for sure, he could not rest. He was constantly on edge. And it showed.

He was drinking a lot more. His men kept a low profile, not wishing to fall prey to his increasingly vile temper.

Somebody must know something. A critter beaten to within a whisker of his life couldn't just vanish into thin air. And who were the skunks that had rescued him?

Questions! Questions! And no answers!

Bowdrie was lying on the bed in his room above the Blue Lagoon. A cigar in one hand, the inevitable tumbler of imported French brandy in the other. Yet even soused up to the eyeballs, the perfidious brain was working overtime.

Snarling, he drew his pistol and fired. Three shots erupted. The mirror at the far side of the room disintegrated into a myriad of tiny fragments. Thin lips bared in a cruel grimace: an ugly smile, cold as ice.

Perhaps there was a way.

Regular visits to the cabin at Gila Bend were fraught with danger. Bowdrie's twenty-four-hour guard saw to that. So trailing out in order to replenish supplies could only be undertaken at night. No more than twice a week. And each time with a different person tending to the injured man's needs. Bronco had insisted that Ellen must remain in Silverton until he was fully recovered. Now that he had found the love of his life, a few weeks of enforced separation were worth tolerating.

As three weeks lengthened into four, Bronco's strength slowly returned. He was able to move around and fend for himself, to cook simple meals and see to his ablutions. Doc Mathers had come out once during this period and indicated his satisfaction with the patient's progress. When asked about the possibility of riding again, Mathers had reluctantly conceded. A tight sling had been fashioned around Bronco's upper body to support the broken ribs which still ached abominably, even though they were knitting together sufficiently well.

It was his right hand that bothered Bronco. Though it looked more like an eagle's talon, he was able to hold light-weight items. It would take many months to heal properly, and then be little more than a tiresome appendage.

Awareness of this was extremely irksome. How could he call Bowdrie out with a broken gun-hand? There was only one solution.

A left-handed draw!

Having reached this conclusion, he asked for a dozen boxes of .44 cartridges to be in the next pack of supplies. In the meantime, he began practising with the other hand. Changing the habits acquired over the last few years in a matter of weeks proved to be a slow and frustrating business.

In the time it takes to say *Death Rides Alone*, two of Bowdrie's hard-boiled rannies burst through the door. Guns at full cock, their feverish eyes swept the room.

Bowdrie emitted a harsh chortle.

His first remark was to Gomez. A rasping growl, low yet menacing.

'You been watchin' that livery man, Mex?'

Gomez stiffened. He hated being labelled. But when Jack Bowdrie was talking, it was best to bite your lip — for the present anyway.

'What he been doing then, *señor*?' sang out the little man.

'That asshole has taken a sudden interest in riding north towards Red Mountain Pass. When the boys stopped him, he claimed he was off to do some trout-hookin'.'

The Mexican's face puckered questioningly but he remained silent.

'Now what d'you suppose he would be needin' to take along for a fishing trip?'

Gomez pondered the query.

'Rod and tackle, bait?' He gave a bemused shrug.

'Right in one!' exclaimed Bowdrie slapping his thigh. His next utterance was preceded by a lopsided grimace. He prodded a finger at Gomez. 'So tell me this. Why does he need a big freight wagon?'

The second hardcase, a flame-topped giant by the name of Texas Red, earnestly considered the poser. Then he proffered a measured suggestion.

'Maybe the guy is thinking to catch a heap of fish.'

Gomez was unable to stifle a harsh guffaw. Red Tucker might be a tough *hombre* in a fight, but he was no brainbox.

A swift cuff from Bowdrie sent the Mexican's sombrero skittering into a far corner of the room.

'This is no blasted laughing matter,' yelled the gang boss, drilling his confederates with an icy glower. 'And anyway, the best fishin' is south of town along the Animas. No! That no-account shit-shoveller is up to somethin'.'

Bowdrie was pacing the room, eyes glowing red with anger. His thick eyebrows met in a ribbed frown. The two bodyguards nervously kept a close eye on the .44 wafting in the air like Monday's washing. He finished the throbbing invective with a final blast from the pistol. The water jug erupted in a shower of coloured fragments. 'And I intend finding out exactly what that is.'

Texas Red waited for his ears to stop ringing before tendering a further nugget of carefully honed opinion.

'So why wasn't the jigger followed to see where he went.' It was a statement rather than a question.

Bowdrie sighed with exasperation.

'Don't you think I figured that one out? The sneakin' jackass must have a sixth sense.' His harsh voice chafed with feeling. 'Gave us the slip every time. Now he's gonna spill the beans.'

'When we do thees, *señor*?'

Bowdrie dug a timepiece out of his vest pocket and flipped open the solid gold lid. A popular ditty tinkled out. Nevada Jones had hocked his most valuable possession some months previously for liquor money.

Redemption had proved to be an illusory dream due to the exorbitant interest charges levied by its now proud owner.

The watch read 9.38 in the evening.

Outside, darkness reigned supreme. A bank of drifting cloud blotted out the moon's radiant glow. The perfect opportunity. It was Saturday night. Murphy always preferred to work late in order to have the next day off.

The gang boss reloaded his revolver, his face a brooding mask. After sinking a final belt of brandy, he slammed out of the room. Falling in behind, his *compadres* exchanged meaningful glances.

Neither would have wished to change places with the ostler for a mountain of silver.

Murphy smiled. He was carefully grooming a splendidly proportioned piebald stallion he had only recently acquired from Clint Weaver at the Rocking-Chair. Powerful muscles rippled beneath the animal's lean contours. He would make a perfect entrant for the annual horse derby run every year down on the flats. The ostler ran a brush lightly over the sleek coat. Perhaps this would be his year.

The horse gave him something else to occupy his mind.

All this business with the young gunslinger was wearing him down. And now his only daughter had admitted to becoming enamoured of the guy. A pinched frown traced a furrow across the raw-boned features. Murphy was worried. So far he had managed to evade any attempts made to follow him on his supply trips to Gila Bend. But sooner or later, Bowdrie was bound to cotton on. Then where would he be? Stuck between the devil and the deep blue sea.

By assisting with the rescue and concealment of the fugitive, he had effectively thrown in his lot with the other side. There was no going back now. He patted the horse, gently blowing into its nostrils. The mount responded with a discerning whinny.

A wistful cast in Murphy's eye was replaced by cold frigidity. A stiff finger traced a line down the yellow scar on his face. Jack Bowdrie's reign as overlord of Silverton had to be terminated. The bastard was bleeding the town and its residents dry. Only yesterday the Mexican, Gomez, had enjoyed informing him that site rental for the stables was being raised. Yet again. That was the second time this year.

'Damn ornery sons of bitches!'

The bitter exclamation spewed from tight lips.

'What was that you said, Dad?'

Ellen Murphy emerged from the back office buttoning her coat.

'A mite tired, that's all,' he countered, quickly reasserting his normal languid expression.

'I'm shutting up now,' she said fixing her bonnet after locking the office door. 'When can I expect you home?'

'Apollo here needs another fifteen minutes. Then I'll settle him down. Don't fix any supper for me,' he added, affectionately tweaking the stallion's pointed ears. 'I'll get something at Lily May's.'

'Don't be late,' Ellen chided lightly. 'Remember, I want to set off at first light for Gila Bend.' This was her first visit to the hidden valley since that awful night a month before. She was anxious to see Bronco. And nothing her father could say would change her mind.

Just like her late mother, thought Murphy. Determined and stubborn, yet at the same time totally devoted and affectionate. He tried to conceal an anxious frown, his watery gaze following her disappearing back. His first consideration was for Ellen's welfare. And if this young man could make her happy, then he had no option but to see this business through to the bitter end.

Whatever that might entail!

Twenty minutes passed. A night owl swooped low over the stable, sharp eyes probing for its supper. In the background could be heard the unremitting jangle of another Saturday night in Silverton. Ben had locked up and was making his way across the rear corral. It offered a short cut to his house. And Blair Street on a Saturday night was always best avoided.

Blessed with a perceptive reaction to night sounds, Ben sensed a disturbance in the ether behind and to his left. There came a stifled cough, the squeak of new leather boots. He paused, right hand dropping to the gun on his hip. As he turned on his heel, opaque shadows suddenly loomed out of the murk.

'What the heck. . . ?'

A heavy thud rammed into his head. For a brief instant, bright lights fizzed and crackled. Then a black hole opened up, plunging his stunned brain into oblivion.

The satin complexion had assumed a wan pallor. For the sixth time, Ellen Murphy opened the door and peered out into the sombre gloom. Even after stopping off for a bite to eat at the Wyman, her father should have been back an hour ago. Had he been detained, he would have let her know, somehow. That was his way: always particular with his time-keeping, Ben Murphy expected the same in others.

So where was he?

Another fifteen minutes passed before she made a

move. Donning a coat and hat, she left for the stable. A complete search of the premises showed it to be empty. Next stop, Lily May Clanton's. Saturday night and the place was heaving. Even so, the hostess made time for her young friend.

The two had hit it off right from the beginning. An age-gap of twenty years only seemed to strengthen their relationship. Lily May was the mother Ellen had never known. And the older woman revelled in her unfamiliar role.

She immediately sensed Ellen's concern. Dark circles ringed the young woman's emerald eyes. Her hunched shoulders indicated some traumatic occurrence. Drawing her into the back parlour, Lily caringly sat the girl down and made her sip a small brandy. Unused to the hard liquor, Ellen was overtaken by a bout of coughing. But it helped to concentrate her thoughts.

Lily May waited, allowing the girl to pick her own moment.

'It's Dad,' she blurted out after composing herself 'He's disappeared. Has he been in here?'

'Not tonight.'

'He told me not to make supper as he'd be eating here.' A choking sob broke from the elfin mouth. 'You haven't seen him, then?'

Lily shook her head. Her heavily painted face creased in thought.

'Let me ask the customers,' she offered. 'Somebody might have seen him.'

Leaving the girl, she returned to the front room.

'Now listen up, you bunch of misfits.' The strident command instantly brought the rowdy eating-house to order. Having gained their attention, she posed the question.

'Has anybody seen Ben Murphy this evening?'

Mutterings and burbled comments followed.

'Ain't nobody clapped eyes on him?' she repeated, scouring the assemblage for some positive illumination.

More murmuring wafted across the overheated room, but nobody offered a way forward.

Lily May cursed volubly. Her straining bosom trembled and shook, much to the enjoyment of the ogling diners. They relished one of Lily May's outbursts almost as much as the victuals. Just to feast their peepers on Lily's more than abundant assets was every man's fantasy in Silverton. A cut above the standard array of saloon gals whom boom towns attracted, Lily May Clanton exuded class but remained a working girl at heart.

'Don't nobody know nothin?' she yelled glaring fiercely at the gaping faces.

A momentary silence, then a small weedy jasper at the back piped up.

'I seen Mr Bowdrie and two of his boys heading that way around a quarter before ten.' Quickly he hurried on, not wishing to appear disloyal to the gang leader should any of his underlings be present. 'Like as not he was collectin' his cayuse.'

The proprietor picked out the black-suited weasel and screwed him to the chair. Wiping at his shrewlike mush with a napkin, Lancelot Spedding, the undertaker, nervously returned her stare.

'Jack Bowdrie, you say?'

'Yes, ma'am.'

The large clock on the wall said 11.30 p.m.

Lily May huffed some, shook a little more, then swung around and returned to the parlour. Inside, a grim seed of impending disaster clutched at her vitals. Outside she remained calm, inscrutable. The unflappable hostess.

'You stay here while I pay the mayor a visit,' she said to Ellen. 'He might have some news. In the meantime, you need to eat. Keep your strength up. I'll get Charlie to fix you something.'

'I'm not hungry,' said Ellen, her satin features pale and drawn.

'All the same, you will eat something.' Lily's tone was final, brooking no dissent.

Ellen merely offered a vague nod.

After passing the order to the cook, Lily May departed. Ellen was left struggling to retain her sanity in the light of what she knew in her heart was the worst possible conclusion. Bowdrie had discovered her father's complicity in Bronco's disappearance, and would do anything to extract the truth. Even down to murder.

Whatever her father revealed, Ellen was certain the gang boss would kill him. There was no way Bowdrie could allow the man to go free. Ben Murphy was a doomed man.

The appalling notion was too much to bear. Ellen burst into tears.

In all her finery, Lily May Clanton stalked up to the ornamental front porch of the mayor's grandiose brick-built mansion. The largest house in town, fronted by a well-tended lawn, it provided a more than fitting residence for Silverton's leading citizen. She gave a hefty rap on the polished oak door. After the second such assault, the door opened and the mayor peered out, suspicion written across his forehead. On seeing Lily, his florid countenance blanched white as a ghost.

His mouthed dropped open.

'Lily!' Fear lent a tremulous edge to the exclamation.

116

'What brings you out here at this hour?' Shiftily scanning the street to see if anyone had witnessed the visit, he quickly ushered her into a side room.

'Is that someone at the door, Dan?' The haughty enquiry emanated from another room close by.

'Just a boy delivering a package,' he shot back, praying the lie would satisfy his obdurate spouse. 'I just need to check the contents.'

'Well, don't be long. I'm going to bed.'

'I'll be as quick as I can, dear,' he called back, exhaling with relief. Then he turned to Lily. 'You shouldn't have come here. If anybody finds out—'

'Don't worry. Nobody will.' The interruption was laced with irony. 'I took great care not to be seen. We couldn't have the good citizens of Silverton learning that their respected mayor was having an affair, now could we.'

'Keep your voice down,' Tanner snapped, grabbing her arm.

'Don't talk to me like that, Foxy Tanner,' retorted Lily vehemently, snatching her arm away. 'All it needs is a scream and your world comes tumbling down. Elizabeth is only upstairs, remember.'

'Y-you wouldn't.' Tanner's nervous inflection betrayed his uncertainty. This feisty woman who had everything his dull wife lacked was capable of anything.

'Try me.'

Their eyes locked. It was Tanner who looked away first.

'So what is it you want?' The acerbic bite had dissolved.

'What has Bowdrie done with Ben Murphy?'

Tanner stiffened. 'What do you know about that?'

'Answer the question!'

'I-I don't know what you mean.'

The abject toady's hesitant reaction spoke volumes.

Lily sucked in her breath ready to emit a piercing shriek.

'All right, all right,' surrendered Tanner, both hands raised. He paused to draw breath. 'They suspect him of having something to do with George Coward's disappearance. Bowdrie intends finding out where the kid is holed up. Then he can get rid of him once and for all.'

'And what about you, Dan. Where do you stand in all this?'

Her voice was flat, an even monotone.

Tanner rung his hands. His blunt features shrivelled. A haunted cast was reflected in the watery eyes.

'I didn't mean for things to go this far,' he whined. 'I always regretted not standing up to Bowdrie when he first arrived.'

'But you were prepared to accept all the trappings, the power and prestige.' A steely edge had crept into her voice.

'Don't you think I know that? But once you've committed yourself, joined the good times, that's it. Like signing a pact with the devil. The only way out is in a pine box.' Tanner seemed genuinely distressed.

Lily sensed her lover's dilemma. She herself had been more than happy to accept the presents he lavished on her, including the dress that now adorned her buxom figure. Specially imported form New York City, it had cost a small fortune. It was just one of a dozen such that now hung in her boudoir.

But if it came to the crunch, would the guy choose between her – ex-saloon girl made good – and the dowdy Mrs Tanner? On that subject, Lily May held grave reservations. She moderated her tone.

'So where do we go from here?'

'I honestly don't know.' Tanner was totally deflated. He slumped into a chair, hands shaking uncontrollably. No longer was he the confident businessman who had so attracted Lily May in the beginning. Nevertheless, she still carried a torch for Foxy Dan Tanner, albeit one emitting a rather feeble glimmer at the moment.

Out in the hall, a clock tolled the midnight hour. Gently laying a hand on his silvery thatch, Lily left without another word.

There was no doubt in her mind that Ben Murphy was either dead, or soon would be. The only problem was how to break the distressing news to Ellen.

TEN

IN THE OPEN

Sunday dawned hot and sticky, living up to its name. Not a breath of wind tempered the arid heat of midsummer. Above the crenellated ramparts, a golden glow heralded the rising of the sun. Purple faded to pink which gave way to a brilliant azure firmament, the perfect backdrop for another day in the Colorado Rockies.

Inside a small abandoned mining level some five miles south-west of Silverton, the new day was not a welcome arrival for Ben Murphy.

His head throbbed. The aching scalp was thickly matted with dried blood. He emitted a painful groan as a lump hammer beat out reveille on the inside of his skull. Struggling to raise himself, he fell back, realizing that he was securely pinioned with rough hemp.

'Has thee stable gringo come round yet?'

The casual enquiry from Gomez received a brusque rejoinder from Butte Madison.

'Go stir him up if'n you feel the urge to find out.' Butte

120

poked at a small fire trying to liven it up sufficiently to brew a pot of fresh Java. 'I got better things to do.'

Gomez bristled. This wet-assed kid had only just joined up with them, and already he was pushing his puny weight around. The Mexican stood up, loosened his revolver in its holster.

'It ees not nice for you to speak like that to your betters,' he hissed, the sibilant murmur barely above a whisper. The meaning though was clear enough. Except to Butte Madison.

'Just eat that shit you call food, Mex, and button up.' He placed a pot of water on the flickering blaze.

Shit? Mex? Madre de Dios!

Gomez's red face swelled at the insults to both his cooking and his heritage. With a roar, he went for his gun. Just in time, the third man around the fire clamped a firm hand solidly over the Mexican's half-drawn pistol.

'Don't be a fool, Gomez.' Buck Flannery issued a calming directive placing himself between the two guntoters. Crossed peepers gave his face a permanent leer, hypnotic and deadly. 'One blast in this rotten cesspit of a mine and the whole lot will be down around our ears.'

Gomez grunted. The anger was still there but now under control.

'Some day, kid,' he spat, flecks of spittle dribbling down his chin, 'when thees business it ees over, you and me . . . we sort things out, *sí?*'

'Any time . . . Mex,' scoffed Madison, nonchalantly pouring himself a cup of coffee.

A loud crack from the rear of the chamber found the trio scurrying over towards where their prisoner was lying. Having attempted to rise, Murphy had pulled loose one of the ancient support beams.

'See what I mean,' snapped Flannery. 'Sooner we get this dude to spill the beans the better.'

'I'm with you there, Cross-Eye,' agreed Butte, flinging the dregs from his cup into the fire. 'And there's no time like the present.'

He slammed a bunched fist into Murphy's face. The man's head cannoned into another beam, scarlet gushing from a split lip. Two more followed in rapid succession.

'OK, mister,' snarled Madison, hauling the ostler to his feet. 'Where have you hidden that bastard Travis'?'

Summoning up a mouthful of saliva, Ben heaved a lump of red phlegm into the young tough's scowling face. Madison howled and grabbed a hunk of timber. He would have stove Murphy's head in if Flannery hadn't shouldered him aside.

'I know a more persuasive means of making thee gringo talk,' said Gomez extracting a red-hot brand from the fire. He waved it suggestively in front of Murphy's bloated features. 'Weel thees change your mind, *hombre*?'

Macabre shadows danced across the back wall of the mine, performing a grisly minuet of death. A cold smile played over the Mexican's face as he waved the searing ember over the exposed torso of Ben Murphy.

A piercing screech rent the static air like a choir of tormented banshees. Murphy fell back gasping for breath.

'Well, *señor*? The hideout if you plis.' The odious grin never wavered.

Murphy shook his head.

Again the brand did its hideous job. A sickly smell of burning flesh filled the confines of the small chamber. Madison gagged, struggling to retain his breakfast.

Gomez chuckled obscenely.

'Too much for you, kid?' He was enjoying himself. 'Eef

you cannot take thee heat, stay out of thee kitchen. Isn't that what they say?'

'This guy is one tough dude,' observed Flannery, with a measure of respect after another hour of brutal torment. They were all sweating profusely in the close atmosphere. 'Let's take a break. Give him time to think about what's in store if'n he don't talk.'

Nobody objected, least of all Ben Murphy. To the ostler, Flannery added: 'This ain't gonna get any easier, mister. And there's no way we can report a failed operation to Mr Bowdrie. He'd skin us alive. Be easier on everybody if you was to tell us want we want to hear.'

For the first time, Murphy opened his bruised and cracked lips. A choking hiss gushed forth.

'I'll see you all in hell first.'

Butte Madison roared impotently and swung another haymaker into the mashed visage. Then the three hard-cases moved over to the fire and some welcome coffee laced with a liberal measure of whiskey.

Through the mist of pain that tormented his abused body, Ben Murphy struggled to comprehend how he had come to be marooned in such a situation. Where had his life gone wrong? Was it the arrival of the young avenger who had so captured his daughter's heart? Or was his stubborn resistance a challenge, a mulish determination to thwart Jack Bowdrie and all he stood for – the mangy cur's arrogant assumption that he could control everything, and everybody.

Perhaps he would never know. Certainly if he didnt extricate himself from his current dire circumstances, and soon, his life on earth would most assuredly be forfeit. But there was a glimmer of light at the end of the tunnel.

Unbeknown to his inquisitors, Murphy's bonds had

worked loose during the gruesome session. At the time he had been too weak and creased with pain to realize it. But now, left to gain some measure of recovery, however slight, he felt his tortured muscles moving more freely. Keeping a watchful eye on the mumbling trio by the fire, he had soon completely wriggled out of his bindings.

But how was that going to help? There were three of them, and he was severely enfeebled. It was a problem that required a swift solution if he was to survive. He would have to persuade one the hardcases to leave. Then he could take care of the other two. Catch them off guard.

Trying not to make any jerky movements that might draw unwelcome attention from his three captors, Ben gently felt around behind his back for a suitable weapon. Every strain on his aching muscles was sheer agony. Then his hand fastened on to a hunk of wood.

It was now or never!

'OK,' he called lifting himself to a sitting position. 'You win. I'll tell you how to find the hideout.' The pronouncement emerged as a choking rasp. His throat felt like sandpaper.

Buck Flannery tossed the dregs of his coffee on to the fire and ambled across.

'Now that's good thinkin', feller.' He nodded sagely. 'No sense puttin' yerself through hell fer nothin'.'

'The problem is,' continued Ben, dragging the words out slowly, 'I only went there in the dark, and used a map that Travis gave me. You'd never locate the place without it.'

Flannery tensed, suspicion making his eyes swivel ponderously.

'So where is this map?' he grunted.

'Top drawer of the desk in my office back at the livery.'

124

'He's stallin',' snarled Butte, hauling out his smoke-pole. 'I say we plug him now.'

'It's the truth,' pleaded the ostler. 'One of you will have to go get it.' He eyed them gingerly through the hazy ochre. 'What would I gain by lying?'

Gomez stroked his stubbly chin. The beady eyes narrowed to thin slits.

'If thees ees a joke, *hombre*,' he bristled, 'You I will enjoy skinning alive.'

Flannery turned to Butte. 'Leather that hogleg and hit the trail. It shouldn't take you more'n a couple of hours to find the map and get back here.'

'Why me?' queried the belligerent young gunman.

' 'Cos I said so. Now git!'

Gomez backed the order with a cold glare.

Madison stood his ground, then complied with a few surly grunts.

The two hard-nosed toughs returned to the fire and an unfinished breakfast. Murphy gave them ten minutes. Then he asked for a mug of coffee.

Flannery brought it across. The ostler tensed, every sinew wound tight as a drum. This was it.

Do or die.

But he was going to die anyway if he did nothing.

The big man bent down offering the mug to his lips. Summoning all his strength, Murphy whipped the club round in a taut arc. A jarring stab lanced down his arm. But his aim was judged to perfection. The bludgeon struck the hardcase on the side of the head, knocking him out cold. As he fell, Murphy grabbed the shooter from its holster and triggered a quick shot at the rising Mexican. The first one chipped a flake of rock off the cavern wall inches from his bullet-like head.

125

Gomez sprang aside, his own weapon palmed in an instant.

Only with a supreme effort of willpower was Murphy able to recock the heavy Remington and loose off a telling shot. He had the satisfaction of seeing Gomez crumple, a crimson hole blossoming dead centre of his forehead.

As the numbing reverberation faded, an eerie silence followed. Then he heard it. An ominous creaking as the old mine timbers shifted. A death knell. Any minute the whole lot could collapse, entombing him within its silvery entrails. Realization that such a catastrophe was imminent spurred Murphy to action. With a speed born out of sheer desperation, he dragged himself into the open, and just in the nick of time.

Behind, a fearful crashing heralded the total collapse of the mine's rotting innards. Ben Murphy attempted a baleful smile. It made a fitting grave for Cross-eyed Buck Flannery and the Mexican.

Fresh air washing over his bruised face was an immediate tonic to Ben's jaded senses. Grateful at having escaped a grisly demise, he gave his oxygen-starved lungs a treat. With the sun high in the wide blue yonder, he reckoned it must be around noon. So how long had he been held captive?

There was no time for idle speculation. Ben was fully aware that his daughter would be in grave danger once Bowdrie discovered his plans had gone awry. Nevertheless, it took him the better part of fifteen minutes just to mount one of the horses tethered outside the mine. Murphy surveyed the landscape, attempting to suss out where it was that he had been incarcerated.

All around, fractured layers of rock poked at the sky, bleak and wind-swept. Below stretched an endless swath of dark green where massed ranks of pine stood to attention. A thin trail disappeared into the gloomy depths. He figured that Silverton must lie to the north, and not too far if Flannery's comment had been correct.

He nudged the cayuse down the tortuous trail. Immediately he was swallowed up in the sepulchral gloom. He shivered in the cool greenness of the forest; partly as a reaction to his recent sufferings, but mainly because of the knowledge that a terminal showdown with Jack Bowdrie was inevitable.

The rosewood stock of a Winchester carbine poked from the saddle boot. And he had the Remington tucked into his belt. Enough firepower to take out Butte Madison should they meet. Such a prospect left him decidedly nervous. Ben Murphy was no gunslinger. His preferred hope was to locate a side trail, so as to avoid any gunplay from which he might well end up as buzzard bait.

It was not until late afternoon that he came in sight of Silverton. Thankfully he had managed to avoid a brush with the young hardcase. Doubtless by now the Kid would have cottoned to the fact that his *compadres* were dead and the prisoner had vamoosed.

At least one thing was in his favour. The gang still did not have any notion as to where Bronco Travis was recuperating. If Murphy could find some place to rest until nightfall, he could slip through town unobserved and make for Gila Bend.

But where to hole up?

Then it struck him. Nevada Jones and his weird sidekick. They had a shack this side of Silverton, tucked away amidst the chaos of the new diggings.

Old Virg's eyeballs popped when he opened the plank door of the two-roomed shack. Hopping about on his spindly pins, he called to his partner.

'Hey Nevada, git yer ass out here double quick.'

The usual half-witted remarks from the old miner were forgotten as he helped the ostler into the spartan living-quarters. Murphy slumped into a home-made chair. He was totally whacked. Virginny poured him a handsome measure of moonshine. The rough edge of the hard liquor seared his throat, but at least it helped revive his wilting constitution.

Jones emerged from the back room, stretching the stiffness from his ageing bones.

'What's all that caterwaulin' fer,' he grumbled. 'Cain't a guy enjoy some proper shut-eye once in a while.'

Nevada's eye followed the direction of his partner's pointing finger. His sagging jaw scraped the dirt floor.

'What happened to you?' he exclaimed. 'Looks as if a stampede of longhorns ran you down.'

'It's a long story,' mumbled the ostler.

'We got the time.' Jones sat down in the other chair.

'No we ain't,' responded Murphy with feeling. 'Ellen will be worried sick that I didn't come home last night. Bowdrie tried to make me tell where Travis is hiding. I escaped before they could force it out of me.' He scrambled unsteadily to his feet, eyes blank and staring, shoulders heaving. Shock was setting in fast. 'I need to see Ellen. If that bastard gets his hands on her, I'll . . . I'll—'

'Hold on there, Mr Murphy,' interjected Nevada grabbing him round the middle before he fell down. 'No sense in gettin' all het up.' Gently he led the injured man into the back room and pushed him down on to the worn flock mattress. 'You need this more than me. A couple of hours' sleep won't hurt none if you say Bowdrie ain't any the wiser.'

Murphy was too far gone to resist. He was asleep in the flick of a rattler's tongue. Jones covered him with a patched quilt then returned to the main room. He took hold of the stone jug and tipped a generous measure down his gullet.

'Well Virg, old pal,' he proclaimed, levelling a solemn look at his partner. 'We sure have gotten ourselves into some bad business here.'

Virg returned the gaze with a profound nod.

'We surely have, Nevada. We surely have'

They both sat down, legs raised on the rickety old table, jugs close to hand. A thoughtful silence descended on the bizarre scene as protesting brain-matter rumbled into motion.

Several noggins later and they had worked out a tentative plan of action.

ELEVEN

ENVOYS OF HOPE

While the ostler was asleep, Nevada Jones slipped into town to seek out Doc Mathers. The medico was enjoying his usual evening tincture at the Starlight House, one of the more genteel hostelries on Empire Street. As Jones stumbled through the door, a myriad of disapproving frowns swung his way. This place was a far cry from the rowdy establishments on Blair. He quickly removed his battered hat.

This watering-hole sure was one classy joint. Crystal chandeliers replaced the smoky coal-oil lamps he was used to; there was a thick carpet instead of sand on the floor; and floral wallpaper rather than the lurid depiction of some scantily clad calico queen graced the walls. The scruffy miner stood in the open doorway. Feeling as out of place as a whiskey drummer at a temperance meeting, he shuffled his feet uneasily.

Nobody moved. A stunned silence prevailed. You could have sliced the atmosphere right down the middle. The respectable citizenry of uptown Silverton were unused to having their salubrious emporium invaded by the common riff-raff.

It was the doctor who broke the embarrassed hush.

'Good to see you, Nevada,' he announced jovially, beckoning the miner over to join him at the bar. 'And to what do we owe this unexpected honour?'

A babble of doubtful murmurings broke out among the assemblage.

Nevada gratefully accepted a tot of the finest Scotch whisky and knocked it back in one. His eyes rolled in appreciation of the choice nectar. Then he drew the medico to one side, out of earshot of the other barflies.

'Ben Murphy is sore in need of your ministrations, Doc,' he stuttered. 'He's ended up on the wrong side of Bowdrie's skulkin' gorillas. They've done him over real good. Afore comin' here, I put him to bed down at my place.' Jones threw the room a suspicious glance to ensure nobody was eavesdropping. Another slug of Scotch vanished down his throat. 'But he's worried about Ellen. Thinks she's in danger herself now that they've sussed him out.'

Doc Mathers stiffened. 'Ellen came to see me yesterday when Ben never returned home. She figured he was dead, according to what Lily May Clanton had told her.'

Nevada offered a quizzical frown. What had Lily May to do with all this? He shrugged.

'Would have been too if'n he hadn't escaped from where they was holdin' him,' he replied. 'Up in the mountains someplace.'

'I'll get down there pronto,' stated the medico, 'and reassure him that Ellen is safe out at Gila Bend.' He sank the last of his Scotch, then headed for the door, commenting: 'Once Lily had wised her up, Ellen went out there straight away to warn Travis. Lily told her to stay put until she could send word as to the truth of the matter.'

Jones could contain his curiosity no longer.

'What's Lily May Clanton got to do with all this?' he asked.

The medico pondered the question as the pair walked back towards the centre of town.

It was not his business to divulge the goings on among his patients, many of whom were also friends. But this was nothing to do with patient confidentiality. And the miner was an ally. Although the old dude hailed from the other side of the tracks, Mathers was sure he could be trusted.

'Lily and the mayor have been conducting what you might call . . .' he hesitated, '. . . a private liaison.'

'You mean Foxy Tanner is havin' a bit on the side.' Jones's face split in a malicious grin. 'That jumped-up connivin' toady. Does his wife know?'

Mathers blustered some, shaking his grey head, but couldn't resist a knowing smirk of his own.

'Lily can wheedle anything out of him,' he said, ignoring Jones's question. He extracted a cigar from his inside pocket, and lit up. A smacking of the lips by Nevada was not lost on the medico. He passed one to the miner then continued: 'She forced him to come clean. The guy didn't know where Bowdrie had taken Ben, but he was sure it was for no Sunday picnic. He intimated that Ben's future was not looking very rosy.'

'And Miss Ellen told you all this?'

Mathers responded with a brief nod.

'What are you going to do now?' he asked.

Jones thought about it. Miss Ellen had a right to know her pa was alive and being cared for. But the miner knew that he could never find his way out to Gila Bend in the dark. Then he remembered that it was Sunset Johnson's old place. The swamper would have to be persuaded to guide him there.

'Tell Old Virginny that he's gonna be actin' nursemaid fer the next couple of days. I'm headin' out to Gila Bend. Them folks need to know what's been happenin'.'

'Well, you take care,' urged the doctor. 'Bowdrie has eyes in the back of his head. And he's hell bent on ridding himself of young Travis.'

It was approaching ten o'clock that night when Nevada Jones and Sunset Johnson eventually reached the cabin at Gila Bend. A coyote howled at the moon. Far away up the valley an owl hooted, its haunting notes floating on the light breeze. The velvet curtain drew down on another day.

The news imparted by the two visitors was received with a sense of relief, tinged with anger that Ellen's father had been so badly treated. They talked well into the night. Bronco was all for setting off there and then to call the gang boss out; settling this business once and for all.

The others urged caution.

'Jack Bowdrie is no pushover,' stressed Jones.

'Yup,' agreed Sunset, 'And he's just brought in another five gun-hands from Durango. You ain't got a snowball's chance in hell of takin' him out on yer lonesome.'

Ellen chipped in from a woman's angle.

'And you're nowhere near fit enough to ride all that way then tangle with a gang of hardened gunfighters.' She stroked a lock of hair from his forehead. 'I have no intention of losing you now. Not after all we've been through.'

Bronco twisted round, smiling at this angel sent from heaven. He winced at a poignant reminder of his precarious situation. His ribs had knitted together, but they still ached. Frustration etched dark lines across his young face.

'Guess you're right.' He sighed, slumping back in the chair. 'So where do we go from here?'

No replies were forthcoming.

Soon after, they decided to turn in for the night. A new day might offer the solution.

And it did!

Sunset Johnson proposed that he should return to Silverton and let it slip that Bronco was holed up in Gila Bend. Bowdrie would then waste no time in heading out this way to finish him off.

This suggestion elicited a chorus of protestations.

'There are only three of us agin at least eight hard-boiled gunmen,' objected Nevada, shovelling down a plate of beans.

'Don't forget me,' chided Ellen vociferously, her emerald eyes flashing, 'I can shoot a rifle as good as any man.'

'Still leaves us a heap of guns short,' added Bronco.

'Let me finish, won't yuh!' Sunset speared them with a punishing glower. He turned to Jones. 'They tell me you was an explosives feller during the war.'

'And since,' agreed the miner proudly. 'Brought down a few rock piles chasing the yellow stuff, I can tell yuh.' His eyes misted over. 'There was that time when Old Comstock asked me to—'

'Later Nevada. OK?' Sunset's butting-in brought a sheepish grin to the old-timer.

'Just recollectin', that's all.'

'As I was sayin',' resumed Johnson. 'I've lived up here for a good few years so I know the terrain like a dog knows its fleas. If we set charges at either end of the gorge into this part of the valley, we could bottle them varmints in—'

'Then pick them off one by one.'

Nevada's eager interruption found the others sitting up, keenly attentive, focused. A new vigour had revived their lethargic minds, a fresh impetus that might possibly find a way out of the impasse in which they now seemed trapped.

Maybe this scheme could work.

'One problem,' cut in Ellen Murphy.

The others eyed her uncertainly.

'It wouldn't work if Sunset here passed the word.' She hesitated, knowing her next comment would touch on a sensitive issue. 'It has to be somebody whom Bowdrie would have no qualms about taking seriously. No offence, Sunset,' she hurried on, wishing to placate the ex-chicken-farmer, 'but you aren't exactly the most respected guy in town these days.'

Nobody answered. They all knew she was right. Especially Sunset. Ellen patted his arm, trying to soften the unwelcome truth.

A hangdog expression came over Johnson's face as he pondered his lowly status.

'Yer right,' he agreed at last, with a heavy sigh. 'Who's gonna take any notice of a saloon cleaner?'

It was Bronco who tried to inject a cheerful element into the dark cloud that hung over the swamper.

'Don't worry, Sunset,' he said brightly. 'When this business is settled, we'll fix this place up and soon have you runnin' the fowlest operation in the state.'

They all laughed at the joke. Even Johnson managed a tight smile.

Then Bronco brought them back to the matter in hand. His next remark was aimed at Nevada Jones.

'So that leaves only you to tempt Bowdrie and his nest

of vipers into this trap.'

Jones shrugged helplessly. His gnarled features remained blank. He had no more influence than Sunset Johnson.

It came as a surprise when Ellen spoke up. 'I'm the one who should return to Silverton.'

Bronco's response was immediate and emphatic.

'Not a chance!' He was not about to place his new-found love in the lion's den.

'Think about it,' she persisted, holding them with a resolute gleam in her eye. 'If I can persuade Lily May to help, she could pass the word to Foxy Tanner. And believe me, she has that squirming jackass wrapped round her little finger.'

Bronco's obvious concern registered on his taut features. Hooded eyes darkened with fear. What Ellen said made sense, although he was loath to place her in any danger. He rose to his feet, ambled over to the rusting stove and poured a mug of coffee. His mind was swimming, in turmoil.

The others waited, and watched.

Outside a lone rooster strutted past, his tail feathers twitching. He was a proudly arrogant defender of the few remaining hens. Against all the odds, this noble creature had managed to retain his spirit of enduring commitment.

The evocative sight galvanized Bronco into action. Now that Ben Murphy had thrown in his chips, the responsibility for upholding the frontier traditions of decency and order rested on his young shoulders.

He was still not happy about allowing Ellen to return to Silverton and a potentially lethal situation. Having been left in no doubt what a headstrong and determined girl she was, Bronco was sure she would take the opportunity

136

to visit her father. And with Bowdrie's sidewinders on the alert, anything could happen.

But if the gang leader was to be made to pay his dues in full, then it seemed to be the only way forward. He turned and gave a diffident nod of agreement.

A collective sigh drifted on the morning air.

'If that's settled, then there's no time to lose.'

Ellen busied herself with preparations for the half-day trip. Sunset went over to the barn to saddle up the black.

Within the hour, Ellen was astride the prancing stallion. She bent down, offering a smooth cheek to her beau. Bronco avidly sought her full lips. There was no restraint. It was a tender moment that passed all too soon. He fervently prayed that many more would follow in the days and years to come.

Ellen spurred off down the valley with a wave of her wide hat, splashed across the creek and was soon lost to view amidst the stand of tall pines.

TWELVE

BAITING THE TRAP

The damask curtains were drawn tight. An orange glow from the single oil-lamp played seductively across the upstairs boudoir. Heady perfume suffused the potent atmosphere, purposefully orchestrated to entice the fly into the spider's web. In this case the poor sap was Foxy Dan Tanner. And reclining on the large four-poster bed Lily May Clanton lay in her most alluring négligé.

A tentative knock on the door announced the arrival of the victim.

'Enter,' came the purring response.

Tanner slid round the corner quickly, shutting the door behind him. A bunch of red roses was clutched in his hand.

'For me?'

Lily rose in a single fluid motion and glided over. Her rouged lips lapping at the mayor's face sounded like a catfish on a slab. Tanner's breath came in short gasps.

'You look divine, my dear,' oozed the mayor, his hands desperately seeking out the lady's more prominent attributes. This was his first visit to Lily May's establishment since their last sensitive meeting at his own house. There was no doubting that he had missed her tender ministrations.

Lily gently but firmly slid from his grasp and guided him to a chair. The last thing she wanted was for her paramour to dally over long. Since learning from Ellen Murphy that Bronco Travis was recovering at Gila Bend, and that she was to be a prime mover in Jack Bowdrie's downfall, Lily had been considering how best to achieve the desired outcome.

She could just blurt it out. Trust to luck that the uncharacteristic change of heart he had exhibited at their last meeting was still ongoing. Could a leopard truly change its spots? In Foxy Tanner's case it was unlikely. The mayor of Silverton was well named. A wily and unscrupulous schemer, he could change with the wind. No. The best way was through the hold she exerted over him.

Her feminine wiles.

'Not just now,' she fluttered coyly. 'We will have plenty of opportunities for that a little later.' The whole purpose of this charade was to encourage him to deliver the news that Jack Bowdrie was so anxious to learn. But he was almost slavering at the mouth, pawing at her like a rutting stag.

Three glasses of champagne later Lily May had cooled his ardour sufficiently to broach the subject.

'There's something I think you should know,' she announced in a hoarse whisper.

'Why does nothin' ever go right fer me?' Jack Bowdrie was ranting at Butte Madison. 'All I ask is for you to persuade a guy to spit the griff. And what happens?' He threw his arms up in despair. 'Two more of my men killed, and that bastard Murphy on the loose.'

'It weren't my fault,' whined Madison, 'He said he had a map showin' the way to where Travis was hidin'.'

'And you believed that load of eyewash?'

'How was I to know he'd jump Cross-Eye and the Mex,' blubbed Madison. He was almost in tears. Ranged behind, the newly arrived gunslingers sniggered aloud. 'Soon as I found the mine had collapsed on them, I hightailed it back here.'

'You shoulda kept on ridin',' snarled Bowdrie. With slow menace, he hauled out his pistol.

'I'm sick of havin' trash like you on the payroll.'

'Please boss, give me another chance.' Madison knew that he was pleading for his life. 'I won't let yuh down again.'

But the gang boss had no intention of plugging the cringing youth. He was already short-handed, even with the new arrivals from Durango.

That was when Dan Tanner burst through the door. He was sweating buckets having run all the way from the Wyman.

'I've just found out where Travis is hiding out,' he panted. A fit of coughing overtook the blunt announcement. Eventually he blurted out: 'He's holed up in Sunset Johnson's cabin at Gila Bend. Nevada Jones is also there, nursing him back to health.'

'How d'yuh find this out?' queried Bowdrie, his tetchy growl laced with suspicion.

'I have my sources,' replied Tanner with a certain reticence. 'But I can tell you that this is one hundred per cent genuine fodder.'

Bowdrie grunted. At the moment, he didn't care about

the source. All that mattered now was that he could finally stick that interfering no account where he belonged – in boot hill.

Bowdrie slapped a balled fist into his open palm. A jaunty air had suddenly lifted the gang boss's previously taciturn demeanour. He felt a weight had been lifted from his shoulders. A fiery glint of revenge ranged behind the black orbs. Flat Nose Jack Bowdrie was ready to kick some ass.

'Saddle up, boys,' he ordered, briskly twirling the revolver in a dextrous manoeuvre designed to impress his new recruits. 'This is when you fellers earn your pay.'

Madison's prospective demise was forgotten, and the kid was more than grateful for Dan Tanner's timely intervention. Now perhaps he could really show the boss that his gun hand was just as deadly as that of any Durango hardcase.

Tanner was unsettled by the influx of so many gunslingers into Silverton. Jack Bowdrie was becoming far too powerful, too conceited, overconfident. And the mayor was beginning to wonder how far his ambitions would spread. Pretty soon he himself might become surplus to requirements, a thorn in Bowdrie's side, a boil to be lanced.

A cold shiver rippled down Foxy Tanner's spine while hot beads of sweat prickled his forehead. He was sorely in need of a distraction. And Lily was still waiting. He hurried off towards the Wyman and the captivating delights of the upstairs boudoir.

A rethink of the situation persuaded Bowdrie to rein in his thirst for vengeance. No sense blasting off half-cocked. First light was the best time for a surprise visit to Gila Bend.

141

*

Ellen arrived back at the cabin as the sun was setting. Lengthening shadows washed over the valley bottom, creating an opaque illusion of uniformity. A flat landscape devoid of texture and vitality. She slumped against the door-jamb, heart pounding, breath pumping in short staccato gasps. Her hair was dishevelled, the satin texture of her face ashen and drawn with fatigue.

Bronco ushered her to a chair, a mug of strong coffee to hand. Even for a man, the return journey from Gila Bend to Silverton in one day was no mean undertaking. It was ten minutes before she felt sufficiently recovered to relate her adventures.

'Soon as I reached the outskirts of Silverton, I took one of the back trails.' She began sipping at the hot Java. It helped revive her spirits. 'With my hat pulled low and jacket collar raised, nobody paid me a second glance. There were no problems getting in touch with Lily May. And she was only too pleased to help out.' Ellen smiled at the recollection of how Lily had intended to bait her trap. 'Believe me,' she spluttered, 'Foxy Tanner has no chance where Lily is concerned.' A thoughtful cast drifted over her serene countenance. 'Although I still reckon she has a soft spot for him.'

'How d'yuh figure that?' asked a sceptical Sunset Johnson.

Ellen threw him an enigmatic look.

'I could see it in her eyes.' She winked mischievously. 'A girl knows these things.'

'Did you manage to bring the goods?' It was the ever-pragmatic Nevada Jones who impatiently brought them back to the present.

Ellen smiled. 'In my saddle-bags.' She nodded towards the door.

Jones emitted a grateful sigh and immediately went outside.

'How is your father?' asked Bronco, thick eyebrows merging in a serious frown. The smile faded from Ellen's face, replaced by a sombre melancholy.

Bronco placed a comforting ann around her heaving shoulders.

'He'll live,' she sobbed, dabbing at her eyes. 'But the doc says he'll be crippled for life. You should have seen him. Poor Dad!' Then the tears came flooding out. But just as quickly, a steely glint bathed her distraught features, the hopeless expression soon turning to a look of cold fury. 'Those sons of the devil will pay dearly for what they've done to us.' She turned to Bronco, ruthless determination written over her face. 'After all this is over, you'll have to stay and run the business. We're both depending on you now.'

Bronco peered long and deeply into the haunted pools of despair.

'I ain't goin' no place,' he said firmly. 'It seems as if we've both got powerful reasons for sending Jack Bowdrie on his way.'

'I hate to break this up, folks,' interrupted Johnson, 'But when do you expect them to attack?'

Bronco scratched his head. 'The way I figure it, Bowdrie won't risk a night ride through Red Mountain Pass. He isn't as sure of the trail as you.' This to Sunset Johnson. 'So I figure he'll reach the entrance to the valley round about noon tomorrow. That gives us ample time to set the charges and take up our positions on either side of the gorge.'

The door opened to admit Nevada Jones.

143

'This should do nicely.' A grin the width of a prime cheese split the miner's rugged features. In his hands rested a dozen sticks of dynamite. 'What more perfect opener to set the party off with a bang.'

It was still dark when the bunch of ten grim-faced gunslingers kicked off next morning. A dust cloud pursued them down the main street as they pushed north for Gila Bend. In the lead, Jack Bowdrie sat tall in the saddle, confident in the knowledge that his control over the mining town was soon to be restored. The elimination of this irksome tinhorn might even strengthen his hold over the miners.

A malicious grin spread like a cancer beneath the black moustache. Nobody challenged Jack Bowdrie and lived to spread the gossip.

THIRTEEN

INTO THE JAWS

Ellen Murphy had roused the others from their slumbers even before the rooster was able to announce his raucous presence. Slivers of pale grey seeped through the windows as the false dawn struggled over the eastern rim of serrated peaks. They yawned, shrugging off the stiffness of night as a new day shyly spread its fingers across the land.

Following a hearty breakfast of ham, eggs and fried potatoes, washed down with a gallon of coffee, Jones primed the explosives with fuses set to go off at fixed intervals. All of them checked their weapons, including Ellen, who had no intention of being left behind. This time, Bronco uttered no objections. It would have been useless anyway. The girl was a free spirit and nothing was going to distract her from the arduous task ahead.

Soon they were heading for the upper rim of the red sandstone mesa overlooking the narrow gorge restricting entry to Gila Bend. Johnson led the way in single file. In this terrain, he felt confident, totally at ease. At first there was no trail. They pushed through the thick stands of pine until the ground began to rise. Here a thin track wound steadily upwards over increasingly rough terrain, eventually breasting the plateau some 300 feet above the valley.

Below, the deeply carved trench of Gila Bend stretched away to the north, the top end lost amidst shattered cliffs of red and orange where the tree-line ended. Johnson pointed his mount south along the rim of a constricted ledge. Clumps of juniper clung precariously to the rock face, their flaky tendrils reaching out to ensnare the unwary. Barely six feet wide, it was a heart-stopping experience, with certain death the result should one of the horses lose its footing.

None too soon, they emerged on to the flat-topped mesa that surmounted the narrow gorge. Here Johnson signalled a halt.

Now it was Bronco's turn to take the reins. He scanned the gorge below for any sign of Bowdrie and his gunhawks. No tell-tale wisps of dust towards the south indicated their imminent arrival.

'How many sticks d'yuh figure will block the ravine?' he asked Jones. The old-timer's experience on numerous prospecting missions marked him as the expert when it came to setting explosives.

Jones took his time examining the cracks and fissures that scored the fractured mesa surface. Too much and they could all end up shaking hands with the devil. Too little and their quarry below would be let off the hook. He prattled and muttered to himself weighing the odds carefully, working out the best places to secure the dynamite.

The others watched and waited, silently urging him to make a decision.

It was Johnson who broke the silence.

'We ain't got all day,' he grumbled. 'Them varmints will

be on us afore you can say boo to a dancing rattler.'

'Can't be rushin' this business. Dynamite is tetchy stuff. Give you a powerful headache if'n you git the fixin' wrong.'

Jones probed a bit more before he was satisfied. Then he set his charges with appropriate timer-fuses located in crevices some ten feet below the edge of the mesa for maximum impact. 'As we agreed,' he told them. 'I've set a charge at each end of the gorge to trap them inside. Then we can pick them off at will.'

'That's the theory anyway,' observed Bronco. 'Let's hope it works out that way.'

'And remember,' Nevada's insistent tone held Bronco with its abrasive edge, 'this needs to be perfect. We don't want any of them assholes slippin' through the net. Too early and they'll have time to back track out of the ravine. Too late and they get through the other side. We have to trap them inside. And we only have two hundred yards to work with.' He pinned the younger man with his searching gaze. 'So don't set off the charge until you see my signal. Savvy?'

Impressed with the old miner's attention to detail. Bronco gave an obedient nod of understanding.

'There are two sticks left,' added Jones, handing one to Bronco. 'Just in case them critters need some extra persuasion to bite the dust. Now find yourself a handy perch at the mouth. I'll take the north end.'

'What about us?' enquired Ellen, levering a shell into her carbine.

'You and Sunset take the middle. Soon as they're in the net, get them shootin' irons a-pumpin'.'

'And make every bullet count,' added Bronco for good measure.

They settled down to wait.

It was approaching the noon hour. Overhead, the golden orb shimmered in a cloudless sky. The only shade was provided by stunted juniper bushes clinging to the rising cliff face, set back from the edge of the mesa. Bronco arranged for them to take turns keeping a weather eye open for the signs of dust drifting above the green canopy below. With only one canteen of water each, he prayed that their sojourn would not be overlong.

'How long d'yuh figure afore we git there, boss?'

Madison had taken it upon himself to ride up front alongside Bowdrie. The gang leader peered down at the map he had been given by Foxy Tanner. It was one that had been specially prepared by Sunset Johnson. He squinted, eyes narrowing to absorb the lie of the terrain. He pointed at a prominent finger of rock.

'That must be Indian Rock up ahead. We're gettin' mighty close, boys. So keep yer eyes peeled and yer guns handy.'

Bronco was dozing, his eyes closed to shut out the sun's unrelenting glare. He untied his neckerchief and wiped the sweat from his sizzled brow. Man, it sure was hot. Ellen was holding up fine beside him. Neither had spoken for some time. The heat was too exhausting.

At that moment he was jolted from his reverie by a dig in the ribs. Johnson pointed to where Nevada was gesticulating with his rifle.

This was it.

On all fours, the three of them scuttled over to the rim of the gorge. Bronco slithered to the southern edge of the mesa where his charge was set. Peering over the rim, he could see that the gang had reined up about 100 yards from the entrance to the gorge. He silently urged them onward.

Five minutes passed.

Then the leader nudged his mount forward at the walk. The other riders fell in behind, their rifles drawn and resting conspicuously across saddle horns. Jack Bowdrie knew they were closing on their quarry and was exercising caution. Bronco breathed deep.

Even from this distance he recognized his adversary, the large powerful body, dark and swarthy beneath the black Texas high crown. And he still sported a thick moustache. Bronco's knuckles whitened as he gripped the Winchester tightly.

At the constricted entrance to the gorge, Bowdrie drew to a halt. They all dismounted. Entering the confines of the gorge, the gang spread out, keeping their distance from each other.

Any minute now. Bronco glanced along the rim, making sure he had Nevada Jones in sight.

Then it happened.

An ear-shattering crump and the far end of the mesa exploded outwards. Boulders of all sizes rained down to block the far end of the gorge. The ground shook with the force of the explosion. Bronco's head spun. This was his first experience of the power that dynamite could exert. It was an awesome sensation.

Soon after, above the grumbling roar of rocks clattering in wild abandon, he picked out the frenzied scream of Bowdrie ordering his men to withdraw. Turning tail, they made a hurried retreat back towards the southern entrance where daylight beckoned like a shining beacon.

That was when the signal came.

Hand trembling, Bronco lit the seven-second fuse. Without waiting to check its course, he quickly scrambled to his feet and raced away from the edge towards the middle section of the mesa where Jones waited with Sunset Johnson and Ellen. As he dropped behind a sheltering boulder the opposite end of the mesa suddenly buckled, the complete southern flank shearing away to topple over in like manner.

Now the trap had been well and truly sprung.

The entire gorge was like a bubbling cauldron, steaming and hissing as clouds of smoke and dust funnelled up from the chaotic mêlée below. It was like a scene from the devil's inferno. Growling and rumbling like an angry bear, the mass of dislocated rock shifted and groaned, then finally settled.

Shouts and curses hailed from the opaque depths of the gorge. Men tried desperately to scramble up over the shifting mass of boulders.

'Let 'em have it,' yelled Bronco, levering his Winchester as the dust cleared.

The others needed no second bidding. Four long guns hammered away, picking off the ants scurrying about in a blind panic. Nobody spoke. Only the harsh grating of leathery throats as the adrenalin coursed through their veins. Lever and fire, lever and fire. The hard crack of continuous heavy rifle fire made their ears ring, eyes stream. Their heads swam under the constant buffeting, shoulders ached with the brittle recoil. Blue smoke twisted and squirmed from hot barrels, mingling with the acrid stench of burnt cordite.

Hard-boiled gunmen though they were, the Bowdrie Gang stood no chance against such an unremitting assault from above.

With nowhere to shelter, the encounter was soon over. Nine men lay dead, their life blood staining the sandy bed of the gorge.

An eerie calm settled over the grim scene. One minute there had been a cataclysmic battering of the senses, the next a mind-numbing silence, intangible yet very real in its intensity. Especially to Ellen Murphy. As the gruesome reality of the situation set in, her whole body began to tremble uncontrollably.

To the men, sudden violence was no stranger. But to Ellen, it came as a brutal shock when she realized that she was now tainted with the blood of dead men. Evil and devoid of pity they may have been, but God's creatures none the less.

Clutching her stomach, she retched violently.

Bronco rushed across, holding her tight until the traumatic reaction had subsided.

'Where's Bowdrie?'

The blunt question chopped through the enveloping silence like a hot knife through butter. Worried eyes swivelled in Nevada's tired sockets.

'He ain't down there!'

'He has to be,' asserted Bronco, unable to take in the import of what Nevada was hinting at. 'Nobody could have lived through that.'

'Come over here and take a gander,' invited Nevada, squatting on the lip of the mesa. 'I count nine bodies down there. And Bowdrie ain't among them.'

'He's right,' agreed Sunset.

Bronco scurried across the flat red slab. He stared down into the abyss. Jack Bowdrie had escaped.

The realization stunned him into silence. He slumped to the ground. Surely, after all they'd been through, it wasn't true. He looked again. But it was.

Jack Bowdrie had slipped through the net!

'Maybe he's hidden by the rocks.'

'Maybe.'

But Nevada's agreement lacked any conviction.

'Let's take a look-see.'

Sunset Johnson made to descend the shattered remnants of the southern flank of the rock face. The others followed slowly, careful not to dislodge any of the loose debris.

The search did not take long. It was soon obvious that Jack Bowdrie had indeed secured the welcome services of Lady Luck. He had somehow managed to evade the hail of lead poisoning that had polluted the ravine. And was still at large. The awful realization found them palming revolvers, anxiously scrutinizing the shadowy recesses amidst the chaotic spread of broken rock.

'Like as not he's hightailed it back to Silverton,' Bronco speculated, eagle-eyes still sifting every nook and cranny just in case the elusive bad ass was playing possum.

But the ex-gang leader had fled the coop.

'You reckon?' from Johnson.

Bronco nodded. 'My guess is he'll cut his losses. Grab what *dinero* he had stashed away and head for pastures new.' His grey eyes hardened. A cold implacable determination shuddered through the rangy frame. 'But that bastard ain't gonna escape again. I'm goin' after him.'

Ellen cried out. Even after the close proximity of death in all its ugly finality, the girl's main concern was for this resolute young man. She clutched his hand with an impassioned concern born out of a regard that transcended love. The anguish that clouded her dignified beauty required no spoken word to convey her fears.

He held her gaze, floundering helplessly in the limpid waters that threatened to overflow.

'It's something I have to do,' he said quietly yet firmly determined.

She understood.

'I'll take one of their mounts.' He only hoped that Bowdrie had been in too much of a hurry to scatter them.

FOURTEEN

TWIST OF FATE

Cursing aloud, Bowdrie took his frustrations out on the unfortunate bay mare he had commandeered after extricating himself from the ravine. Savagely digging the silver rowels into the mare's flanks, he spurred the horse to greater speed. The sooner he reached Silverton the better.

It had been his intention to leave the mining town in the near future. Just not this soon. How had that son-of-a-bitch known he was heading for Gila Bend? It didn't make sense. Bowdrie racked his overwrought brain, struggling to figure it out. Someone must have double-crossed him. The question was who.

Tanner had passed him the word. So where had he found out'? Jack had been so intent on his mission that the notion of a set-up hadn't occurred to him. It had to be a middle man whom nobody would suspect. Somebody in both camps.

Then the solution struck home. Not a man – but a woman!

Lily May Clanton.

She and the Murphy gal were bosom buddies. And

Tanner was having it off with Lily. That sleazy bitch must have fed Tanner the low-down so he, Jack Bowdrie, would ride into an ambush. And it had worked perfectly. Bowdrie howled at the wind, lashing the poor horse with his quirt. He berated himself for a gullible fool.

At least he had managed to slip the noose. Now he had one final task to perform before kicking out for California.

Jack Bowdrie slipped into Silverton unobserved. He felt like a skulking rat instead of the much feared and respected hard-ass he had aspired to be over the last eight years. Was this what his life had become? And it was all down to that kid? Perhaps when things had settled down, he could return and finish the job once and for all.

He who turns and runs away, lives to fight . . .

Behind the Wyman Hotel, he drew the exhausted bay to a shuddering halt. The distraught animal could barely stand. White foam oozed from every pore. Bowdrie checked his twin revolvers. Both were fully loaded. The ambush had been so sudden that he had not even managed to return fire.

After glancing round to ensure he was alone, Bowdrie quickly scooted up the back stairs, entering the hotel on the upper floor at the far end of the corridor. Nobody was about. He checked his timepiece. It was early afternoon – 2.15 p.m. That two-faced whore ought to be resting in her room after the lunchtime rush.

Slowly he moved down the corridor. Hers was the room with the polished mahogany double doors. Pausing outside he cocked an ear, listening. A low steady murmur alerted his senses. His teeth bared in a twisted smile. She was taking a nap. This called for the silent approach. Gunplay was out. Returning the six-shooters to their holsters, he extricated a stiletto from his boot.

Twisting the brass handle he pushed the door gently. Unlocked, it swung open accompanied by a grating squeak. Lily shifted her position on the bed. Her eyes fluttered open. All she could see in the half-light were a pair of black eyes bearing down on her. Glinting fiercely, they pinned her to the bed with a savagely magnetic compulsion. Then the blade came into view.

A scream formed in her throat.

Bowdrie slipped out the way he had come. His lips formed a cruel grin of satisfaction that revenge had been meted out. Now all he needed to do was reach his office and empty the contents of the safe.

Meanwhile Bronco had made good time. Without any of the stealthy wariness with which Flat Nose Jack had entered Silverton, the pursuer urged his mount to a full gallop down Blair Street, hauling rein outside the Blue Lagoon. Unfazed by the garish appearance of the whorehouse, Bronco walked straight in through the front door and headed for the stairs leading to the upper floor.

'Hold on there, mister,' objected a thin, skeletal dude behind the bar. 'You can't go up there.'

The young interloper paused, an arrogant smirk on his face.

'Why not?'

'Those are the private chambers of Mr Jack Bowdrie and his associates,' smirked the smug stringbean. 'Only specially invited guests are allowed access.'

'Well I ain't special, and I ain't been invited,' returned Bronco placing his boot on the first step. 'But I sure am anxious to make Mr Bowdrie's acquaintance.' It occurred to Bronco that his enemy might well be up there already, just waiting to plug him. In a casual manner he asked: 'Has he arrived yet?'

'No. But I am expecting him at any moment.'

'Then I'll wait upstairs.' Bronco backed up his confident declaration with the drawn Colt.

The stringbean acquiesced with a shrug. He wasn't about to taste a hot lead sandwich for anyone, no matter how well he was paid. Bronco thanked him with a curt nod and went upstairs.

Carefully he checked each room. Two were decked out sumptuously as living accommodation, a third was Bowdrie's sleeping-quarters. It was the fourth that he found most interesting. The office. This was where Bowdrie would come first to secure his ill-gotten gains. He would have hidden all his private papers and money in a secure place where he could retrieve them easily. An iron safe would be the best option. But where was it?

Keeping an ear open for Bowdrie's arrival, Bronco quickly searched the room. There seemed to be no place where any valuables could be secreted. Then he noticed a large picture on the wall. A painting that depicted wild horses being corralled. It brought back vivid memories relating to a part of his life which hadn't been so complicated.

'Nice isn't it?'

Bronco spun on his heel. Jack Bowdrie stood in the doorway, the twin Peacemakers pointing unerringly in his direction.

'So, Mr Coward, we meet at last,' smirked the big man. 'A pity we won't have time to get properly acquainted. Seein' as how you've done fer me in this miserable berg. Good thing I was ready to kick off anyway.' He prodded one of the barrels at the painting. 'If it was my grubstake you were hopin' to filch, then look no further.'

157

Bronco gave him a quizzical frown.

'The safe is behind the picture. I had it specially made in Chicago. A fine piece of workmanship, eh? And only you and me know about it. Ain't that a laugh?' The black moustache quivered as Bowdrie thumbed back both hammers. 'A pity because it's too late for either of us. I'm headin' fer California. And you're hellfire bound to join your pa.' Bowdrie emitted a chilling guffaw at his wit. 'Goodbye, Mr Coward.'

The blast of gunfire echoed round the opulent surroundings. But it wasn't Bronco Travis who chewed lead.

As he was punched forward by the force of the bullets shattering his spine, Bowdrie's arms lifted involuntarily, the guns clattering to the carpeted floor. His legs wobbled, turning to jelly as he keeled over. The strained visage twisted, expressing total confusion at the turn of events. It shouldn't be him that was coughing up his life's blood.

Then a flat, detached voice broke into his jangling thoughts.

'You shouldn't have killed Lily.' Taking a moment to collect his traumatized thoughts Dan Tanner continued, his tone rising as a hate-filled urge took over. 'Leaving me to find a knife in her throat. Now that was the work of the devil himself.' Tears ran down his creased face. The Smith & Wesson Starr clutched tightly in his balled fist shook with his barely suppressed emotion. Bronco could see that the guy was close to breaking up.

Bowdrie struggled gamely to raise himself; his hand vainly clawing at one of the fallen hoglegs.

'It's him what you should be cuttin' down, not me,' he gasped. 'Coward's the one who's threatenin' our set-up here.' The effort to plead for his life lent added strength to his rapidly draining body. The carpet was now a smear of purple. He nodded towards the picture on the wall. Choking breath issued from the open maw in a series of rasping grunts. 'Take what yer want out the safe. . . . It's all yours. . . . But get me to the sawbones . . . I need help bad.' Bowdrie coughed loudly, puking up a vile spume of crimson phlegm.

Tanner laughed. A biting rip that lacked any semblance of humour.

'You honestly think that money can buy what you've taken away.' Heaving sobs racked his lean frame. Dan Tanner was close to the edge.

Bowdrie's hand closed over the revolver. It lifted slowly.

Tanner's face cleared. The pallid complexion was lifted by a merciless glimmer. He uttered a venomous roar and emptied the rest of the Starr's load into the cringing wreck.

The supreme effort had taken its toll. Tossing the gun aside as if it was poison, Tanner dropped into a chair, his head slumped ungainly over his chest.

Caught betwixt life and death, Bronco's heart was hammering against his rib cage like an overcharged steam pump. The thick smoky atmosphere was choking. He needed air. He staggered over to the window, threw it open and breathed in long and deep. He ignored the crowds that were gathering outside the cathouse, attracted by the lethal torrent of gunfire.

Eventually he turned to face the mayor.

'You saved my life, Tanner. I won't forget that.'

Tanner raised his head. Bloodshot eyes, half closed stared back. He wore a thin smile.

'It was for Lily, not you.'

'All the same, I'm beholden.'

'I ought never to have gotten involved with Bowdrie and his skulking ways,' said Tanner, blankly. 'But once

159

you've taken the first bite of the apple, you're hooked with no exit save a one-way ticket to purgatory.'

For ten minutes. Tanner just sat, a dead look in his eyes, He stared blankly at the heap of bloody rags that had been Flat Nose Jack Bowdrie. Bronco leaned against the wall opposite, the tension slowly ebbing from his body as tight muscles relaxed.

Then. Rising slowly to his feet, Tanner smoothed down his frock-coat, picked up the fallen hat and set it at a jaunty angle on his head. Extracting a silver hip-flask from his pocket, he took a long slug. It helped to steady his shredded nerves.

'This marks a new beginning for me, and for Silverton,' he stated with a firm resolve. 'The town needs a hospital, and a school for the kids. With the blood-money I've salted away over the years, and Bowdrie's stash,' he pointed his silver-topped walking cane at the wall painting, 'this town can find its self-respect and make a fresh start.'

Foxy Dan smiled, this time exuding a warmth that had been lacking for too long.

'And we're going to need a new marshal,' he added, lifting a raised eyebrow to the young man. Pretty Boy Gadds might still be at large for all he knew. But his days were numbered, just like any other chancers tarred with the same brush. 'You want to take over where your father left off?'

Take over from his father.

There was nothing more he could have wanted from his return to Baker's Park, which had become Silverton. And the new marshal would need a wife to support him. A sublime expression played over the clear-cut features.

He nodded to the other man offering his left hand.

'You got yourself a deal, Mayor.'